CONTENTS

embrace your inner DAFFODILITY.

Watch every day
on Nickelodeon!
www.nick.co.uk

Pedigree

Published 2010. Pedigree Books Ltd,
Beech Hill House, Walnut Gardens,
Exeter, Devon EX4 4DH.
books@pedigreegroup.co.uk
www.pedigreebooks.com

HOT PROPERTY!

This iCarly Annual belongs to

_ _ _ _ _ _

HOW IT ALL BEGAN!

How did Carly go from being a regular Seattle teen chick to the star of the world's hottest new webshow? It all started with a detention, an angry English teacher and a picture of a rhinoceros...

When Sam decided to photocopy Miss Briggs' head to the body of a rhino, she didn't expect her teacher to go quite so wild! Puckett was in a STACK of trouble already, so Carly had to step in to take the blame. The punishment was harsh to say the least – instead of going to a Cuttlefish concert, Carly was forced to spend her Saturday in detention, running the school's talent show auditions.

Carly wanted to borrow Spencer's video camera for the auditions, but he'd already made it into a model of a squirrel! Desperate, she knocked on Freddie's door. Freddie jumped at the chance of helping out – he'd had a crush on Miss Shay since forever! As she'd been the one who landed her in the mess, Carly dragged Sam along too.

Freddie filmed the auditions, but most of the performances were very boring! The only clips that made him laugh were Carly and Sam's chatter between auditions – especially their comments about Miss Briggs' pointy boobs!

All would have been a storm in a teacup if Freddie hadn't somehow managed to upload Carly and Sam's comments onto SplashFace! Carly and Sam freaked when they realised what had happened!

Fred panicked too, but wasn't able to get the clips back off the net until the following morning. By then, it seemed the whole world (including Miss Briggs) had watched them over and over again.

Even though they were in deep trouble, Carly and her friends were overwhelmed by the positive comments that surfers uploaded. People in their thousands were calling for her to star in a regular webshow. With Sam as co-host and Freddie as tech producer, Carly decided to give them what they wanted!

One crazy hat party and oodles of webisodes later, iCarly is still a top click on everybody's browser. The rest, as they say, is history…

'People over thirty should really not make out.'

'I ain't gonna give you no soup!'

'I'm not laughing. Sometimes my lip just quivers like this.'

'We don't care about taters. Even in tot form!'

HEY THERE.
PEOPLE OF EARTH!

Carly In Person

Carly is a fun-to-know ninth-grader who also happens to be the star of her very own webshow! She lives with her crazy big brother in a cool loft apartment in downtown Seattle. With Freddie across the hall and Sam dropping by every five minutes, no wonder Carly and her website are the talk of the town!

FULL NAME:	Carlotta Shay
BIRTHDAY:	January 14th
STAR SIGN:	Capricorn
FAMILY:	Big brother, Spencer
HAIR COLOUR:	Brown
EYE COLOUR:	Brown
INTERESTED IN:	Cute guys

MAKES HER GO MMMM!: Starring in iCarly, sipping smoothies, hanging with Spencer, going to the movies with Sam

MAKES HER GO EUCH!: Spiders, Nevel Papperman, Sam cutting her toenails on the couch, Lewbert's wart

LOVES: Spencer's Spaghetti Tacos

CARLY TRIVMANIA

- Her dad works on submarines! On his last naval posting, Carly and Spencer lived for a while in Seal Beach.

- She takes vitamins every day!

- Once Carly slow-danced with Freddie Benson!

THE THINGS I LIKE BEST ABOUT CARLY ARE:

1.

2.

3.

SAM'S GOT A LOT TO
SAY FOR HERSELF –
UNFORTUNATELY MOST
OF IT'S OFFENSIVE!

- 'Wutev!'
- 'I'm not a people-person.'
- 'Mama plays to win!'
- 'Suffering from extreme studipity?'

SAM I AM!

Sam on the Cam

Sam Puckett is not the kind of girl you'd like to cross. She's a very determined character with a strong will. Sam's a surprising choice for Carly's best friend, but the combination works. Sam may pick on Freddie, but deep inside Sam knows that it's the iCarly team – and that includes Freddie – that keeps her on the straight and narrow.

FULL NAME:	Samantha Puckett
BIRTHDAY:	April 17th
STAR SIGN:	Aries
FAMILY:	Twin sister, Melanie
HAIR COLOUR:	Blonde
EYE COLOUR:	Blue
INTERESTED IN:	Watching movies, cutting school

MAKES HER GO MMMM!: Bacon, chilling on Carly's couch, Fridays, playing Cupcake Slam, watching crazy iCarly clips

MAKES HER GO EUCH!: Spotting Freddie's mum tucking in his trousers, Miss Briggs playing the bagpipes, detention, hanging out with Melanie

LOVES: Anything meaty

SAM'S YEARBOOK HONOURS MAKES INTERESTING READING:

- Most likely to get suspended.
- Teacher's pest.
- Fastest smoothie slurper.
- Most likely to ask for more food at a party.
- Most likely to be in detention

THE THINGS I LIKE BEST ABOUT SAM ARE:

1.

2.

3.

IN FIVE. FOUR.
THREE. TWO...

ENTER THE
WONDERFUL WORLD OF
FREDWARD BENSON...

'Thank you Carly.
In your face Sam.'

'Buenos dias, muchachalatas!'

'Everyone jokes about the
white balance til the skin
tones go magenta!'

'I'm the best long divider!'

Freddie's Inside Info

Freddie is a sweet, techy kind of guy who only loves one thing more than his laptop – his serious crush on Carly. Freddie's over-protective mum, Mrs. Benson, often shows him up in public, much to the amusement of Sam. Freddie can't think of a better job than being tech producer on iCarly – the greatest webshow on Earth!

FULL NAME:	Fredward Benson
BIRTHDAY:	February 14th
STAR SIGN:	Aquarius
FAMILY:	Mum, Marissa
HAIR COLOUR:	Brown
EYE COLOUR:	Brown
INTERESTED IN:	The latest Pear gadgets

MAKES HIM GO MMMM!: Carly's cute smile, fencing, watching Galaxy Wars with Spencer, speaking random Spanish

MAKES HIM GO EUCH!: Bumping into Sam first thing in the morning, missing AV club, his horrible ex Valerie

LOVES: Popcorn and smoothies

FREDDIE TRIVIAMANIA

- He's extremely allergic to bees!
- His mother gives him tick baths!
- As well as being A/V Club vice-president, Freddie's the High School Debate Club President and a member of the Ridgeway Young Businessmen's Club

THE THINGS I LIKE BEST ABOUT FREDDIE ARE:

1.

2.

3.

SPENCER IS THE CROWN PRINCE OF CRAZY – JUST LISTEN TO HIM!

- 'A monster ate my soup.'
- 'Pyooo. Pyooo. Pyooo.'
- 'She only liked me for my socks.'
- 'I may be an idiot but I'm not stupid.'

MY BABY SISTER IS A WEB STAR!

Spencer's Secrets

Not only is Spencer Carly's cool big brother, he's her guardian too. While their dad is away with the navy Spencer is in charge. There's only one rule in his book – have fun! Spencer is an artist with a wild imagination. If he's not hanging out with his best friend, Socko, he's creating sculptures out of junkyard finds.

FULL NAME:	Spencer Shay
BIRTHDAY:	November 11th
STAR SIGN:	Scorpio
FAMILY:	Little sister, Carly
HAIR COLOUR:	Brown
EYE COLOUR:	Brown
INTERESTED IN:	Cute girls, hot mums, anyone who's single

MAKES HIM GO MMMM!: Playing Pak-Rat, hanging out with Socko, whipping up a batch of tacos, playing with magnets

MAKES HIM GO EUCH!: Being grown-up, adverts for insurance, boring socks, watching a new artwork go up in smoke

LOVES: Mr Galini's Coconut Cream Pie

SPENCER'S BEEN ON LOTS OF DATES. HERE ARE A FEW OF THE MOST MEMORABLE...

- Stefanie. He broke up with her because she was too annoying.

- Veronica. The relationship didn't work because she only liked him when he was wearing a tuxedo.

- Connie. Stopped going out when he realised that she was also seeing other guys.

THE THINGS I LIKE BEST ABOUT SPENCER ARE:

1.

2.

3.

REC●

Hello People!
Draw a picture of
yourself in here or
stick in a photo.

FANZONE

MY FAVOURITE ICARLY EPISODE:
....

THE COOLEST CHARACTER:
....

THE THING THAT I'D MOST LIKE TO SEE HAPPEN IN THE SHOW:
....

....

THE BEST ICARLY VIEWER CLIP EVER:
....

....

Pack the Profile!

The iCarly webshow is 100% interactive – so let's find out all about you too! Use this page to create a profile about yourself. Now's your chance to write down all the things that make you *you!*

FULL NAME: Loryn Jayne Duffus

USER NAME: ?

BIRTHDAY: 24th of October

STAR SIGN: Scorpio

FAMILY: Mum, Dad, Adrian, Jordan

HAIR COLOUR: Dark blonde

EYE COLOUR: Blue

HOMETOWN: Wick

PETS: Foxy, Megara (Dogs)

INTERESTED IN: Animals, Acting

MAKES ME GO MMMM!: 2_ _ _ _ ₪

MAKES ME GO EUCH!: B**** Friends Jelousy

FAVOURITE FOOD: pasta, choco Trifle.

MOST LIKELY TO SAY: ⊕
...Sure...............

................'S

TRIVMANIA

Write some surprising stuff about yourself in here

PEAR PHONE PUZZLE

Some joker has been messing with Carly's new mobile! All her texts have got scrambled so she doesn't know who sent what. Carly needs to get it sorted fast – she's going out tonight and her friends are going to be texting the details!

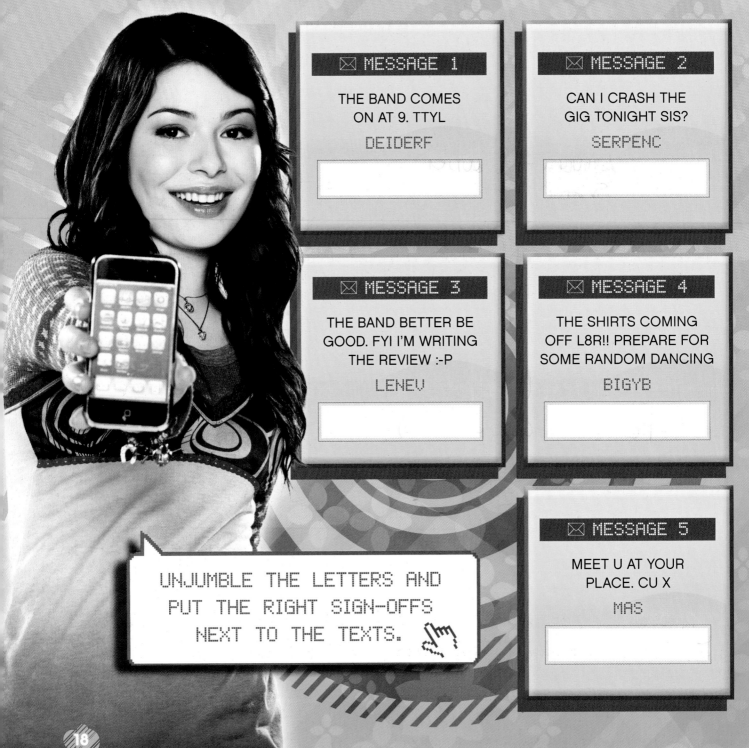

✉ MESSAGE 1

THE BAND COMES ON AT 9. TTYL

DEIDERF

✉ MESSAGE 2

CAN I CRASH THE GIG TONIGHT SIS?

SERPENC

✉ MESSAGE 3

THE BAND BETTER BE GOOD. FYI I'M WRITING THE REVIEW :-P

LENEV

✉ MESSAGE 4

THE SHIRTS COMING OFF L8R!! PREPARE FOR SOME RANDOM DANCING

BIGYB

✉ MESSAGE 5

MEET U AT YOUR PLACE. CU X

MAS

UNJUMBLE THE LETTERS AND PUT THE RIGHT SIGN-OFFS NEXT TO THE TEXTS.

...IT'S CREDDIE!

Carly and Freddie are hall neighbours, web superstars and total pals! Freddie would love to add boyfriend and girlfriend to that list, but Sam is always there to remind him that that won't be happening anytime soon!

Take a good look at these photos that Freddie has uploaded.
Find six differences in the one on the right!

CARLY'S HOT BLOG!

HEY PEOPLE, thanks for checking out my fantastic blog! Now that the jingle bells have stopped jingling at our place for another year, I wanted to tell you about my totally WEIRD Christmas.

It all started with a fire, a wish and an electromagnet Christmas tree. Confused? You will be!

Never one to go with the crowd, Spencer decided to MAKE the tree this year!

He built a 'magnatree' using metal from the junkyard, then bolted a giant electromagnet on the top! I was kind of disappointed.

Even with decorations and all our presents round it, the tree looked as festive as a flagpole in August. That night things got a whole lot WORSE!

Spencer's creation caught fire and all the presents I'd bought for him got shrivelled in the flames.

I was so mad, for one insane minute I wished that Spencer was normal, just like all the other big brothers out there.

That's when something totally FREAKY happened. My guardian angel Mitch turned up to show me exactly what my life would be like if Spencer was just a regular dude. Sensible Spencer was engaged to Freddie's mum, Sam was in JUVIE and I was dating skunk-bag NEVEL PAPPERMAN!

I didn't hang around to see anymore – I wanted my Spencer back! I begged Mitch to give me the guy who makes crazy sculptures, accidentally sets stuff on fire and wears socks that light up!

Who knows if I was dreaming or not web-watchers? All I do know is that I got Spencer and my quirky friends back to just the way I like 'em!

Moral of the story is simple – be careful what you wish for! And never make a Christmas decoration out of a super-conducting magnet!

Carly x

A whole lot of wacky stuff has happened in the Shay household this holidays! Read the speech bubbles then draw lines to the people that said each one.

A SAM

B FREDDIE

1. Come check out our magnetic Christmas tree!

2. It's just I wanted a Christmas tree that smells like Christmas. This smells like junk.

C SPENCER

3. Ho ho ho. Can I walk away now?

D ME

4. If somebody wants to get to the mall in time to sit on somebody's lap and tell somebody what he wants for Christmas, somebody better hurry up.

ACT 'N' UPLOAD!

HERE'S THE TEAM'S QUICK GUIDE TO GETTING YOUR CLIP NOTICED...

BFF

Making the iCarly webshow has taught the gang one thing – it's an insane world out there! Even Sam Puckett's iron jaw has dropped at some of the wild, wacky and downright silly stuff that people like to do on camera.

Have you ever thought of sending in a clip? Whether it's licking a tennis racket or body-popping in your back garden, iCarly wants to hear from you! Here's the team's quick guide to getting your clip noticed...

PICK YOUR ACT

Do you have a secret talent that's begging to be revealed in front of millions of webfans? Take a little time to think about the stuff you do best or take a look at the ideas on pages 80-81.

BREAK SOME BOUNDARIES

Bored of singing, dancing and magic tricks? Carly and Sam totally respect crazy new art forms. Think outside the box, packing your clip full of surprises. Something original and unforgettable will make people come back to see more!

RECRUIT YOUR CAST

You don't have to perform alone if you don't want to! Double the viewing pleasure by roping in a friend, your little sister or even your next-door neighbour. If you're going to act like a goon on screen, it's OK to share the shame!

FIND YOUR LOCATION

Spice up your clip by filming in unusual places. Clips set at the dinner table, on your trampoline or even under the bed will add a surreal new dimension to your performance!

CHUCK IN SOME SPECIAL EFFECTS

Freddie puts his own stamp on iCarly by wowing the viewers with sound effects and super-cool graphics. With a bit of lateral thinking you can do the same on your clip too! Why not add some strange noises or flash a torch to give a disco effect?

MAKE TIME FOR A RUN-THROUGH

The best acts have been well-rehearsed – juggling avocados, doing a slow-motion impersonation of your head teacher or playing music through a kitchen roll isn't easy you know!

ALWAYS
ask your parents' permission before uploading anything on to the web!

BOOK YOUR DIRECTOR

Who's going to be lucky enough to film all this raw talent? Find someone with a steady hand, a good eye for a shot and a very, very open mind!

SEND IT IN!

Visit icarly.co.uk and submit your work!

IN FIVE, FOUR, THREE, TWO...

OK, here's the boring stuff. If you want to be in with a chance of getting your clip on the iCarly site or even the show you need to:

1. Say your first name and your age, then step back and do your thing!

2. Don't say or do anything bad (nothing mean, no bad words). Don't do anything dangerous. Make sure your clothes don't have logos or bad words on them either.

3. Don't say or show full names, school names, cities, street names, phone numbers or email addresses.

4. Try to keep your act shorter than three minutes.

5. Don't include music in your clip. But, if you're dancing and you want to include music, that's OK. Never talk if music is playing.

iSaw Him First

When Freddie's friend Shane turned out to be a total hottie, Carly and Sam had a fight on their hands...

Sam walked across Carly's kitchen and then slid a drink across the table to her friend. Carly took one look at the glass and groaned.

"What's wrong?" barked Sam, flipping a cashew nut into her mouth.

"You asked me what I wanted to drink," said Carly. "I said 'ice and lemon'."

"Oh," Sam frowned. "I forgot the ice."

Carly slapped her forehead. "And the lemon!"

Before Carly could ponder why she kept inviting Sam over, the apartment's elevator pinged. The door opened to reveal Spencer suspended between two floors. It must have been the third time that the lift had got stuck in a week.

Spencer crouched on all fours and peered through the bottom of the elevator.

"I've had it!" he bellowed, waving at Carly like a maniac. "Call for help!"

ICARLY WAS LIVE IN TEN!

Just then Freddie breezed into the apartment – iCarly was going live in ten minutes!

"Hey," grinned Carly. "Where's your tech wizard friend?"

Sam winked. "Yep, where's the nerd?"

Freddie had promised to get one of his pals to lend a hand on the show.

"Just 'cos he's in the AV club," scowled Freddie, "It does not mean that he's a nerd."

Carly and Sam looked at each other. Of course he was going to be a nerd.

The latest episode of iCarly would hit the jackpot on any wack-o-meter in town. For reasons best known to themselves, Carly was dressed in a Hawaiian hula outfit while Sam had kitted herself out in a flared Seventies trouser suit that was totally out there! The viewers loved it.

"Next," beamed Carly, "We will stuff blueberries up our noses."

The girls started stuffing.

"Zoom in on this Fredward," directed Sam. "It's classic footage."

At that untimely moment, Freddie's nerdie pal stuck his head round the door.

Carly and Sam spun around, their blueberries wobbling in surprise. For the first time ever Freddie had brought over a good-looking friend! Sam recovered herself first.

"Let's meet Freddie's nice friend," she beamed. 'C'mere."

Freddie was grossed out. "His name is Shane."

"Shane," whispered Carly. It sounded nice.

"So you're in the AV club with Freddie?" gushed Sam, jettisoning the sad wig she'd been wearing.

Shane flashed a smile so bright the girls thought they were going to pass out.

"What could be cooler than a guy in the AV club?" cooed Carly. "Awesome."

HOLY cheese!

iSAW HIM FIRST

Despite his love of science, Shane turned out to be just as cool as Carly and Sam hoped he might be. The next day at school, all the friends could think about was their gorgeous new webshow buddy.

"Has anyone seen Shane?" asked Freddie, meeting the girls in the hall.

Carly reached for her lipgloss. "Is he coming here?"

"What time?" demanded Sam.

"Calm down," muttered Freddie. "I just need to give him back his flashdrive."

Sam and Carly both dived for the memory stick, landing in a heap at Freddie's feet.

"I'll handle it," sighed Freddie, scooting off. "Crazies."

As soon as he was out of sight, Carly pulled Sam over to her locker.

"Do you think it would be crazy for me to ask Shane out?" she whispered.

Sam suddenly began to study her toes.

"What?" pushed Carly. "You think he'd think I was being too desperate?"

THEY'D BOTH ask HIM OUT!

Carly searched her friend's face. "Tell me what **you're** thinking!"

"I was thinking…" replied Sam. "…about asking him out myself."

"Ulch," moaned Carly. The only way to be fair in these situations was to follow the girl code. Whoever saw Shane first should get to date him. Carly and Sam agreed 100 per cent.

"So I'm gonna ask him out," they both said in unison.

DO THE BELLY RUB!

That evening, the friends got Freddie to cue a tape of the show on the flatscreen in Carly's loft.

"We've got to find out who saw Shane first," said Carly.

A very bored Freddie rewound to the moment in iCarly where the girls first spotted his AV buddy.

"Now play it frame-by-frame," instructed Sam.

Freddie did as he was told.

"A dead-tie," he said flicking a switch at the end of the playback. "So I guess neither of you can go out with Shane. Awww, too bad."

Freddie had officially had enough. He shut down his laptop and rattled down the stairs, passing Spencer who was in deep negotiation with an elevator repairman.

CARLY WAS DESPERATE TO DATE SHANE

"So what are we gonna do now?" asked Sam.

Carly thought for a moment. She **was** desperate to date Shane.

"Who says we can't both go out with him?" she asked. "It's not like we're talking about marrying the guy."

Sam grinned. "OK. And it'll work cos we're best friends."

It was settled. Carly reached into her pocket for her Pear phone.

"I'm going to call Shane right now!" she smiled maturely.

Sam smiled right back, waving the mobile she was after in the air.

"Not without this you're not," she said.

The next day didn't go so well for anybody. Freddie was sick of hearing about Shane and Spencer still couldn't get his elevator to work. The repairman he'd booked had been round for hours. All he'd managed to do was send the lift crashing nine floors down to the basement.

"Can you show me the stairs?" asked the guy, picking up his tool kit.

"Yeah," muttered Spencer. "But only if you promise not to fix them."

WE WILL BE MATURE

Spencer was leading the repairman down, just as Sam was coming up.

"Sorry I'm late," she said sheepishly. "Was getting my homework done early."

Carly was on to her straight away. Sam hadn't done her homework since second grade.

"You can tell me if you were with Shane," she replied casually. "Remember that we're gonna be mature about this."

Sam put her hands up. Not only had she been with Shane, he'd told her that she had a cute nose!

When Carly revealed that she'd shared a smoothie with him the night before, Sam couldn't hide the glare.

ALLEY CAT INSULTS

"You're just jealous 'cos he said I had a cute nose!" she barked.

Before they knew it, the mature friends were trading insults like a couple of alley cats.

"That's it!" screamed Carly. "I'm outta here!"

She started a dramatic walk-out, then realised that she was stomping out of her own apartment. Sam obligingly stormed out instead and slammed the door.

As soon as Carly spotted Sam by the lockers at school the next day, Miss Puckett made it clear that she didn't like being enemies.

"I feel really bad about our fight," said Sam, handing over a plate of made-up cookies.

Carly looked suspicious. "You try one first."

"OK," said Sam, taking a bite of choc chip.

WITH ME OUT OF THE WAY, YOU'D HAVE AN ALL-ACCESS PASS TO CLUB SHANE

When Sam didn't pass out, Carly grinned and took a biscuit.

"Hey, hey, I see cookies!" bellowed Freddie, running across the hall. He prided himself on sniffing out biscuits from 200 metres.

"Sam made them," nodded Carly.

Freddie instantly let the cookie crumbs fall from his mouth.

"Ugh!" he cried. "When was the last time Sam washed her hands?"

Carly and even Sam politely put their biscuits into the bin.

Just then Shane swept into the hall. Sam and Carly gulped. He was looking totally gorgeous **again**!

It was when they both started chasing him down the corridor that they realised that this shared dating thing was never gonna work.

"I've got an idea," said Carly. "Whichever one Shane kisses first gets to date him. He has to kiss one of us, lips to lips."

Sam nodded. The deal was *so* on!

THIS ISN'T A LOOK. IT'S JUST MY FACE.

i Saw Him First

While Sam and Carly got plotting, Spencer was losing it with the elevator repairman.

"How long do you think it'll take before it's fixed?" he asked.

"I dunno," mumbled the repairman, fiddling with a bolt. "Three... or four."

Spencer waited for a little more explanation. Nothing came.

"Three or four what?" he shouted. "Days? Weeks? **Months**?"

The elevator repairman nodded sympathetically. "Yeah. Maybe five."

DON'T WORRY I DON'T WANT TO KISS YOU!

Over at Ridgeway High, Sam was putting 'Plan Shane' into action. She'd knocked up a charity booth offering kisses in return for a dollar. So far there'd been zero takers.

Freddie strolled over. For the first time in weeks Sam looked genuinely worried.

"Don't worry, I don't wanna kiss you," he grimaced. "But I do want you to win this Shane contest."

Sam eyed him up suspiciously. She knew Freddie only wanted her to win so that the field would be open for him to date Carly. It was devious, but so what? Shane was too hot to be allowed to slip away.

Just then, Shane wandered through the hall. Sam sprayed Freddie with a water gun to get him off her back. They would speak later.

"I'd love to help your charity," he grinned. "But I've left my wallet in my locker."

"Bobby!" screeched Sam, grabbing a passing science geek by his shirt. "Lend Shane a dollar."

It was too late. Before Sam could claim her kiss the bell rang and Shane had disappeared into class.

That evening Carly had arranged to go on a date with Shane. She flew round the apartment spritzing perfume and setting out coasters. Everything had to be just right if she was going to get Shane to kiss her.

Shane rang the doorbell at seven. He was looking dreamier than ever!

"If we're gonna catch the movie we should go now," he smiled.

Carly grabbed him by his shirt and pulled him inside.

"Y'know what?" she smiled as innocently as she could. "Let's just blow off the movie and hang out here."

She led Shane to the couch, deliberately nudging him onto a blue folder that happened to be lying there.

"It's just a play that I've written," she said breezily. "I'm going to perform it in class, but I can't find anyone to rehearse it with."

'a chance for romance. an original play by carly shay'

Shane fell for it hook, line and sinker.

Carly miraculously found another copy of the script from under a cushion and within seconds they were acting out the most passionate school play ever!

"Mabel you look so beautiful in the moonlight," murmured Shane.

"Oh Bruno, thanks," gushed Carly, in character.

"You rock for saying that."

Shane looked down at the script. The stage directions called for a kiss.

BRUNO KISSES MABEL FOR AT LEAST THREE SECONDS

Shane gently bent his head, following the script to the letter.

Carly closed her eyes and waited...

"Hey!" shouted Spencer, bursting in and killing the moment. "I made toast by leaving a piece of bread in the sun next to a mirror and some tinfoil!"

i saw him first

By the time it got to Friday, Sam was getting desperate. She and Freddie needed to put into operation their most reckless scheme yet.

At break-time, Sam carefully laid herself out in front of the lockers and closed her eyes. Right on cue Freddie led Shane into the hall.

"What's wrong with Sam?" asked Shane, dropping his bag.

"I don't think she's breathing," claimed Freddie. "You know how to do mouth-to-mouth resuscitation. Take over!"

Shane nodded. "I got a CPR certificate last year."

Sam laid back and prepared to receive the kiss of life!

Just at the wrong moment, a forceful hand shoved Shane to one side.

Sam squinted up with one eye and groaned. Nurse Shrager!

TIME FOR STAGE TWO OF THE PLAN!

Sam opened her eyes properly – the most unsympathetic school nurse in the history of Ridgeway was about to give her the kiss of life! "Wait!" she begged. "I'm feeling better!"

Nurse Shrager was not amused. "I'm gonna report you to the principal for impersonating a sick person! What's your name?"

"Rebecca Berkowitz!" lied Sam, wrestling the nurse off her. Shane and the real Rebecca Berkowitz scratched their heads as Puckett sprinted towards the girls' bathroom.

On Saturday night, Carly implemented stage two of her Shane campaign. She'd invited him over to work on their history project, but she had a very different sort of date on her mind. Spencer had been briefed to stay out of sight so she and Shane could hang out in the iCarly studio.

"The electricity still not working?"

asked Shane, pointing to the candles dotted all over the room.

Carly dragged her beanbag a little closer.

"Yes," she fibbed. "Here have a strawberry."

Suddenly romantic music started to drift out the sound system. Shane gave up and closed his folder.

SHALL WE TAKE A BREAK? I CAN'T SEE MY BOOK IN THIS LIGHT!

Carly nodded a bit too eagerly. Her big moment had to be coming soon! Shane just needed one more little push…

"Ew! There's something in my eye," she said. "Can you get closer and take a look?" Shane bent forward.

"I can't see anything," he whispered. "But…"

"But what?" gasped Carly.

Shane smiled. "You have a really pretty eye."

Carly waited. She was *so* gonna win this contest…!

iSaw Him First

"What up, what up, what up!" shouted Sam, flicking on the light switch. Freddie stood behind her – the great Shane-Carly kiss was over before it had even begun.

"Foul!" complained Carly, leaping to her feet.

Sam walked over and prodded her pal in the stomach. "What foul?"

"You intentionally sabotaged my moment," yelled Carly.

Shane Made a Life-Altering Decision

Shane wisely stood back so that Sam and Carly could have some space to fight. Freddie shrugged and shook his head. "You ruined it on purpose!" accused Carly.

Sam wasn't giving an inch. "I so did not!"

As the shouting got louder, Shane made a life-altering decision. Who would want to go out with either of these crackpots?

"Girls!" he bellowed, calling time on the spat.

I've seen girls get competitive over a guy before but you two are out of control!

Carly and Sam stopped. Shane looked really mad. "I don't know what's up with you two," he said. "But I've had enough of it!" He grabbed his stuff and backed towards the open elevator. Carly and Sam tried to cut in and warn him, but Shane wasn't up for listening.

"You girls call me when you learn to be more…" Shane stepped into the elevator shaft, then dropped out of sight like a rock. "…Maturrrreeeeeee!" The elevator repairman clearly still had some more work to do.

REC

I'M THE BEST LONG DIVIDER!

Shane's little accident taught Carly and Sam a lot about guys **and** open elevator shafts.

"Let's never compete over a boy ever again," begged Carly as she, Sam, Freddie and Spencer stood in Shane's hospital room. The unlucky object of the BFFs' affections lay on a bed with his arms and legs in traction.

"Never," nodded Sam, wincing as the doctor tightened one of Shane's bandages.

HE LOOKS SO... BROKEN

The girls both felt awful. If only Shane hadn't tumbled down the full nine floors.

"He'll be alright," said the doctor.

"How long before he's up and around?" asked Freddie.

"Hard to say," replied the medic. "Could be three, maybe four."

Spencer freaked. "Days? Weeks?"

The doc nodded and carried on writing. "Maybe five."

"Let's go," sighed Spencer. "Who wants food?"

THE HOSPITAL CAFETERIA HAS TURKEY FINGERS

The guys walked out of the door, leaving Shane to sleep.

After a couple of seconds, Carly tiptoed back inside. She bent down and gave the unconscious boy a silent, three-second smooch.

She straightened up and quietly sighed – bliss!

"I win!" she whispered, racing to catch-up with the gang.

CHEESE TEASE

This crazy maze just shows why squirtable cheese should always be handled responsibly! Sam's been going nuts with the snack in a can again, spraying cheese all over a brand new victim. Who's she trying to goo with the squeezy savoury today? Follow the trails until you get to the lucky guy!

START >>>

FREDDIE ☐   GIBBY ☑   LEWBERT ☐

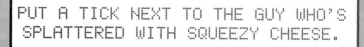

PUT A TICK NEXT TO THE GUY WHO'S SPLATTERED WITH SQUEEZY CHEESE.

CARLY'S WORLD
WORDSEARCH

Wordsearches are for wimps, right? Wrong! Carly's ramped this one up by asking you to guess the word clues as well as finding them on the letter grid. Fill in the eight blanks then circle them in the panel below with a bright pen. Don't forget the words could be running in any direction, including back-to-front!

E	I	H	T	O	O	M	S
U	X	N	E	V	E	L	P
A	A	L	L	Q	X	W	E
K	V	D	T	K	B	V	N
E	Y	U	T	C	I	J	C
T	V	S	A	M	S	U	E
Y	A	W	E	G	D	I	R
O	N	G	S	R	H	S	T

1. Carly's big brother is called _Spencer_.
2. Carly goes to school at _Ridgeway_ High.
3. Carly's dad serves in the US _Navy_.
4. Carly and her friends live in _SEATTLE_.
5. Carly used to have a crush on a hot guy called _Jake_
6. Carly's arch web-rival is _Nevel_.
7. Carly's fave drink is a _SMOOTHIE_.
8. Carly's BFF is called _Sam_

SUPER FAN QUIZ

PART ONE

QUESTION 1 — □ ✕

What is the name of Gibby's pet dog?

Grambles

HOLY CHIZ!

QUESTION 2 — □ ✕

What search engine does Freddie use when he surfs the web?

Zaplook

QUESTION 3 — □ ✕

If she had to pick one word, how would Carly describe Nevel Papperman?

Now that iCarly's biggest fan Mandy Valdez has decided to be a rock band groupie instead, the top spot is vacant! Are you a triv champ who knows the show inside and out? Pit your wits in this two-part challenge, cunningly devised by Spencer to separate the average viewer from the all-time super fan.

QUESTION 4 — □ ✕

What did Spencer quit after just 13 days?

OUCH!

QUESTION 5 — □ ✕

Which host of the webshow controls the sound effects with a blue remote?

QUESTION 6 — □ ✕

What is Freddie and Spencer's favourite space movie?

QUESTION 7 — □ ✕

Who does Sam have a regular Tuesday appointment with?

QUESTION 8 — □ ✕

Which one of Spencer's artworks nearly caused Carly a serious injury?

I'M NOT EDUCATED BUT I'M A WHOLE LOT OF FUN!

QUESTION 9 — □ ✕

What's the name of Sam Puckett's virtuous twin?

QUESTION 10 — □ ✕

What iCarly feature allows viewers to chat with Carly and Sam live on air?

FINISHED?
NOW FLIP TO PAGE 88!

STARRING: YOU!

iGo to Japan

CAST
WRITE YOUR ACTORS' NAMES BELOW!

★ **CARLY SHAY**

PLAYED BY:

★ **SAM PUCKETT**

PLAYED BY:

★ **FREDDIE BENSON**

PLAYED BY:

★ **SPENCER SHAY**

PLAYED BY:

★ **MRS. BENSON**

PLAYED BY:

Carly was totally over-excited when her show was nominated for an iWeb award! When she discovered out that she, Sam and Freddie were invited to attend a glittering presentation ceremony in Tokyo, Japan, the news got a whole lot better! Find out what happened when Spencer and Freddie's mum heard about the upcoming iCarly vacation...

Find some friends and decide what part you should each play, then act out the scene below. You can use props and costumes if you want to, or you could just get into character and read through the script.

Episode 201: iGo To Japan
Act 1, Sc 5 – Carly and Spencer's loft day.

CARLY: Okay, why is it dark in here?

SPENCER: [Out of shot] Because...

[Suddenly a very bright light comes on, surprising the three kids. They all gasp and then Carly turns on the room lights. We see Spencer wearing a construction worker's helmet with a super bright headlight on it.]

SPENCER: [Proudly] I made this!

CARLY: Why?

SPENCER: It's for jogging at night. [Points up at headlight] This baby puts out over 19,000 watts – it could light up a football field.

FREDDIE: For how long?

SPENCER: 'Til this battery runs out.

[Spencer turns to reveal a ridiculously large, heavy-looking battery on his back.]

SPENCER: [Cont'd] I got it out of a car.

[There's a knock at the door. Carly opens it to reveal Mrs. Benson holding a package in her hand.]

CARLY: Oh, hi, Mrs. Benson.

FREDDIE: Mom, what are you still doin' here? I thought you left for your pottery class.

MRS. BENSON: I tried to, but my car wouldn't start.

[Spencer looks away, nonchalantly.]

Episode 201: iGo To Japan

MRS. BENSON: Anyway, I forgot – this package addressed to iCarly came yesterday.

CARLY: [Annoyed] Yesterday?!

MRS. BENSON: I'm sorry, I meant to tell Freddie but…

SAM: [Excited, taking package] Just give it.

SPENCER: Is that from the iWeb Awards?!

CARLY/SAM: [Opening package] Yeah! / Yep!

[Freddie joins Carly and Sam.]

FREDDIE: C'mon, what country are we goin' to?!

[Carly yanks the papers from the box.]

CARLY: Uhhhhh… [Matter-of-fact] Canada.

[Sam and Freddie exchange disappointed looks.]

SAM: [Bummed] Canada?

CARLY: [Grins] Just kiddin' – TOKYO! We're goin' to JAPAN!

[The three kids freak out with excitement and exchange hugs and high fives. Carly hugs Freddie but he holds on a little too long.]

CARLY [Cont'd]: Uh Freddie, you can let go now.

FREDDIE: Oh, right.

[Spencer takes the packet from Carly and looks inside.]

SPENCER: Sweet! Y'know, I took a year of Japanese in college. A little brush up and I'll be speakin' Japanese like a… Japanesiologist.

[Mrs. Benson takes the packet from Spencer and looks inside.]

MRS. BENSON: [Thinking, worried] Freddie, I'm not sure I can allow this…

SAM: [Sighs, annoyed] Here we go.

STOP SQUISHING IT!

Episode 201: iGo To Japan

FREDDIE: Mom...

CARLY: [To Mrs. Benson] It's just Japan.

MRS. BENSON: Right, which is why I worry that... y'know the Far East can be very... [Gives up] Look, just because I can't think of anything right now doesn't mean Japan isn't fraught with danger.

SAM: Ulch, c'mon lady.

SPENCER: [To Mrs. Benson] It's okay. I'm goin' with 'em. So it's not like they won't have a responsible adult making sure everything goes smoothly.

JUST GIMME SOME SOUP!

[Spencer's headlight hat catches on fire which causes everyone's jaws to drop, stunned. Everyone starts screaming! The kids grab some towels and frantically use them to put out the hat fire. Mrs. Benson just watches all this in shock.]

SPENCER: [Cont'd] Put it out! Put it out! Put it out! Please, please, please, put it out!

[When it's over Spencer sits on a stool sheepishly, his hat smoking.]

SPENCER: [Cont'd, but less confident to Mrs. Benson] So I'll make sure everything goes smooth in Japan.

MRS. BENSON: Freddie, you're not going to Japan!

OPPOSITES ATTRACT!

CARLY AND SAM HAVE BEEN BEST FRIENDS EVER SINCE THEY WERE EIGHT-YEARS-OLD. THEIR BOND WAS FORGED WHEN SAM TRIED TO STEAL CARLY'S TUNA SANDWICH AND SHE REFUSED TO GIVE IT UP. NOW THEY'RE TEENS AT RIDGEWAY HIGH AND CLOSER THAN EVER!

Best Friends Forever?

Name: ....

1. Favourite colour ....

2. Best subject at school..

3. Worst subject at school..

4. Most surprising thing about them......................................

5. The song that sums up our friendship ....

....

6. Their guilty pleasure ....

7. Best-ever holiday ....

8. Favourite item of clothing ....

9. Most visited website ....

10. Message they're most likely to text ....

....

AND JUST FOR FUN... ▼

MY THEORY WHY OUR CRAZY COMBINATION WORKS:

Best Friends Forever?

Name: ....

1. Favourite colour ....

2. Best subject at school ....

3. Worst subject at school ....

4. Most surprising thing about them ....

5. The song that sums up our friendship ....

   ....

6. Their guilty pleasure ....

7. Best-ever holiday ....

8. Favourite item of clothing ....

9. Most visited website ....

10. Message they're most likely to text ....

    ....

AND JUST FOR FUN... ▼

MY THEORY WHY OUR CRAZY COMBINATION WORKS:

....
....
....

THE PALS ARE LIKE CHALK AND CHEESE, but somehow the girl-next-door-meets-rebel combo seems to work. They've had some epic fights and been through some tough stuff, but no one can break them apart.

Carly and Sam feel the same about all the important stuff – iCarly, random dancing and spaghetti tacos. Are you and your best friend as close as Carly and Sam? Sit opposite each other, then answer this quick-fire friendship test. If you can both hit scores of six or more – you're definitely buddies with staying power!

¡iOwe YOU

SAM HAD BEEN HITTING HER FRIENDS UP FOR CASH FOR TOO LONG – NOW IT WAS PAYBACK TIME!

Carly and Freddie were chatting in the hall when Sam pulled the friends apart.

"Can I borrow thirty bucks?" she asked. "I gotta pay a cab driver."

She told a story about her mum loaning the Puckett family car to a fisherman. Freddie didn't buy it at all.

"A cab here from your house doesn't cost thirty dollars," he argued.

"It does if you make the guy stop to buy you a breakfast burrito," countered Sam, getting impatient.

C'MON! THIRTY BUCKS – HE'S GOT THE ENGINE RUNNING!

Carly and Freddie sighed, then pulled out their wallets. They could just about scrape thirty between them. Sam snatched the cash then skidded back outside. By the time she got back into school Freddie had got himself all worked up.

"I'm getting a little tired of you always borrowing money," he scowled. "I think it's kinda lame."

Sam pulled a face.

"Maybe I borrow money a lot, but don't I always pay back every…"

"No," said Carly.

"All right. You guys figure out exactly how much I owe you and I'll return every dime," she shouted. Sam stomped off down the hall.

Freddie and Carly raised their eyebrows. They'd have to see, taste and smell the money to believe that the promise had been kept.

46

Later that day, Carly and Spencer were chilling out on the couch when Freddie turned up, armed with his laptop and a bunch of AV cables.

"You ready to rehearse some iCarly?" he asked.

"Yep," nodded Carly. "Sam's on her way too."

The guys were running upstairs to the studio when the doorbell rang. Spencer dragged himself off the couch and slumped over to get it.

"Hello there," said a cute little scout in a yellow Sunshine Girl uniform. Behind her was her even cuter mum.

Spencer stopped slouching and tried to look suave.

"We live down the block," explained the hot mum. "I've been taking Emily round to sell Sunshine Girl Fudge balls."

I LOVE FUDGE BALLS!

"Would you like me to buy a box?" asked Spencer, bending down to greet the little girl with a cheesy grin.

Instead of smiling back, Emily burst into tears and ran down the stairs. Spencer gulped. Was his face really that scary?

"It's not you," sighed the mum. "She's just so shy. She's trying to sell the most Fudge balls in her troop so she can win a really cool bike."

Spencer's mind started to spin.

"I can help her sell 'em!" he offered. "How tall is your husband?"

Emily's mum blushed. "I'm single."

"All right!" said Spencer. "Now I really wanna help!"

than she'd bargained for!
Carly clicked on a
spreadsheet. "Show
her Freddie."
A meticulously
plotted chart came
onto the flatscreen.
Freddie began
to analyse
Sam's out-of-
control debt.
"If you look
at the graph,"
he waffled.
"You'll see
that your
borrowing
really took
off two years
ago during July
and then... ow!"
Sam slammed
shut the laptop
onto his hands.

YOU SQUISHED MY TRACKPAD FINGER!

Freddie cradled his fingers,
getting more and more red-faced.
"Are you going to pay us back
or what?" he demanded.

"I was," groaned Sam. "But I didn't
know it was going to be that much."

Carly got practical. "How
much do you have?"

Sam emptied her pockets. She
was the proud owner of fourteen
dollars, an AA battery, some string,
a fork and a mouldy olive.

Freddie was right. He and Carly were
never going to get their money back.

iOwe YOU

A half hour later, Sam strolled into the
iCarly studio swigging a root beer.

"So Fredward," she said. "Did you figure
out how much money I owed you guys?"

Freddie flipped open his
laptop then booted up.

"You owe Carly and me exactly five hundred
and twenty six dollars," he announced.

Sam spat the rest of her root beer
all over the floor. This was **way** more

Spencer decided to launch his Fudge ball quest with a stand outside the local supermarket. He figured that he and Emily were bound to clean up there!

Emily's mum explained to her daughter what they were going to do, while Spencer set the boxes of Fudge ball flavours out across the table. Before he'd even finished, the little Sunshine Girl got overwhelmed and ran off crying.

"You go and try to calm her down," said Spencer. "I will sort out the Fudge balls."

The first potential customers strolled by. Curiously they seemed to speed up whenever Spencer shouted his Fudge ball sale pitch.

"C'mon," he yelled. "We've got peanut, caramel, marshmallow…"

WHO'S IN THE MOOD FOR SOME FUDGE BALLS?

Before Spencer could close his first deal of the day, two older Sunshine Girls rocked up with a table and two chairs.

"Er girls?" called Spencer. "What's up?"

The girls ignored him, pitching their table right outside the supermarket door.

He tried again. "Maybe you two didn't notice, but I'm set up right over there. I'm trying to help a little girl win a bike."

"Maybe we want a bike too," pouted the tallest Sunshine Girl.

"Here's the thing," said Spencer. "There are not enough customers here for all of us. Since I was here first I was thinkin' that…"

The Sunshine Girls stopped unpacking their box of Fudge balls.

They walked calmly over to Spencer's table, then hurled it out onto the street.

Spencer gasped. There wasn't much sunshine going on here!

49

iOwe YOU

The next day Carly and Sam were well and truly working the camera on the iCarly webshow. Freddie tried not to snigger as the pair goofed around in the studio.

"Hey!" cheered Sam, interrupting their spiel. "I just found a dollar on the floor! Anything can happen on a live webshow."

"Now you just need to find about five hundred more," added Freddie.

Carly stepped forward for a tight close-up. "Sam and Freddie have been fighting about money this week."

"So if you wanna help me out with my little debt problem send me some cash!" quipped Sam. "Care of Ridgeway Middle School here in Seattle."

THEY AIN'T GONNA SEND YOU CASH!

Back at the supermarket, Spencer's feud with the Sunshine Girls was getting pretty nasty.

"I forgive you for what you did yesterday," he generously told the pair, even though they'd set up their pitch right in front of his again. "We do, however, need to talk."

The tall blonde Sunshine Girl looked rather bored, then turned away.

"I was only trying to help a little girl," he continued, putting down his skateboard. "And I don't think it was very 'sunshiny' of you to pick up my table and throw it down the... yah!"

The instant that Spencer dropped his guard, the girls hopped up and shoved him on the back.

"This is not over!" he yelled, spilling Fudge balls all over the pavement.

"Sam!" bellowed Freddie, catching her in the corridor at school. "Principal Franklin wants to see you right now!"

Sam quietly groaned. Which misdemeanour had he found out about this time?

"Tell him I moved to Switzerland," she decided. "I'm gonna make a break for it."

Freddie shook his head. "He's got teachers posted at ever door in the building."

"Tell Carly to meet me at Franklin's office in two minutes then."

"What did you do?" asked Freddie.

"I dunno," sighed Sam, telling the truth for once. "But he always goes easier on me when Carly's around."

an explanation for these? Each of these letters is addressed to your show care of my school! They all contain cash."

Carly picked up a letter, then remembered Sam's plea on iCarly. The viewers must have really wanted to help.

"This is serious," she frowned.

"You cannot solicit money from kids over the Internet. It's illegal," barked the Principal. "I suggest you return it all immediately."

Sam glared at the massive stack of letters. It would take them forever to send that stash back!

IT'S MY BEST FRIEND CARLY WHO LOVES ME AND SEES THE VALUE IN ME AS A PERSON!

Sam and Carly got to the Principal's office at just about the same time. Mr Franklin looked irritable, tapping his fingers and staring at the clock.

"What happened?" whispered Carly.

Principal Franklin tipped a mail sack of letters onto his desk. "Maybe you two have

TTyL

SHAMPOO A SQUIRREL!

iOwe YOU

YOU'RE NOT GOING TO TAKE A NAP WHILE WE SIT HERE MAILING LETTERS!

It took the guys four trips to drag all the mail sacks up to Carly's apartment. Freddie and Carly started fixing on stamps, while Sam printed out address labels. Boring was not the word.

"I can't believe how many iCarly fans sent in money just 'cos we asked them to," said Freddie.

"It's gonna take days to send it all back," agreed Carly. "Sam, how you comin' on with those return address labels?"

"Real good," muttered Sam.

Carly knew her best friend much better than that. She wandered over for a progress check.

"You're not making labels!" she shrieked. "You're looking at trampolines on the Internet!"

The alarm tweaked on Sam's phone.
"I gotta go."

Freddie and Carly leapt up and barred the door.

"I'm not going to take a nap," shrugged Sam. "I got a job at Chili My Bowl."

Freddie was speechless – Puckett had never done an honest day's work in her life!

"Chili?" gasped Carly, suspicious.

"Yeah," nodded Sam. "I figure if I gotta work, it might as well be around something that I love."

Sam skulked out, just as a bedraggled Spencer was skulking in.

"I'm in a bad mood," she muttered, by way of greeting.

Spencer knew that vibe. He'd moved his Fudge Ball operation down to the dockyard and had just been pelted with clams.

Sam hated working at Chili My Bowl. The hours sucked, the uniform was lame and customers were so rude.

"Hey lady," said an obnoxious guy with a mouthful of tortillas. "I said I wanted hot sauce. There was none on my tray."

"Sorry," answered Sam. "Here's some hot sauce."

The man snatched the bottle out of her hand. "You should have put it on my tray in the first place."

Sam smiled sweetly. "You know where I want to put it right now?"

"You watch your mouth!" yelled the man.

YOU WATCH YOUR MOUTH BEFORE I PUT MY FIST IN IT!

The manager of Chili My Bowl stepped in just before a riot broke out.

"Hey!" he frowned. "You say you're sorry to the customer."

Sam started to complain, then forced herself not to swing for the man.

"I'm so… very s-sorry," she stuttered.

The manager nodded, then handed Sam a mop and bucket.

"You've got to behave if you want to keep this job," he announced. "Now go and clean the men's room."

Sam was horrified. A gross dude belched as he made his way into the bathroom, still holding his bowl of chilli.

"Can't ya get a guy to do it?" she pleaded.

The manager shook his head. "Now."

Sam gulped. There was nothing for it – if she was ever going to pay Freddie and Carly back, she had to go in there and get cleaning.

It was pretty late when Sam turned up again at Carly's. Carly and Freddie were still licking and sticking the mail.

"Just thought I'd stop by on my way home from work," said Sam in her most chipper voice. "Oh Freddie, your mum's looking for ya. Something about a sick relative?"

Freddie bolted out the door. Sam's face suddenly fell.

"I just made that up so he'd leave," she explained. "I don't want him to see me cry."

I DON'T LIKE WORKING! THEY DON'T LET YOU SLEEP, OR WATCH TV, OR GO ONLINE

Sam fell onto the sofa in a heap. She sobbed uncontrollably on Carly's shoulder for a full half hour – work just wasn't in the Puckett DNA!

"I can't stand to see you like this," said Carly. "You'll have to quit."

Sam shook her head.

"I can't! I promised I wouldn't quit until I paid every penny I owe you and Freddie!"

Carly sent her friend home to bed. How many more shifts at Chili My Bowl could she take?

CARLY, I GOT BIG NEWS!

Carly didn't expect to see Sam cry and she didn't expect to be woken up by Spencer at six the next morning.

"I've been looking at my law books," he beamed. "It's only illegal to solicit money over the Internet if you don't offer a product or service in return."

Carly shrugged.

"What product can we send our iCarly fans?"

Spencer brought himself up to his full height, uttering just two words.

"Fudge balls!"

iOwe YOU

Carly couldn't wait to get to school the next day. The minute she got out of registration she grabbed Freddie and spilled everything about Spencer's brainwave.

"Fudge Balls?" repeated Fredward. The mind boggled.

"Uh-huh!!" nodded Carly. "Spencer and his mates are posting Fudge balls right now to every iCarly fan that sent us money!"

Freddie thought for a minute. "But wait… Fudge balls aren't free."

"No," agreed Carly.

That was the genius part. When they subtracted the cost of the Fudge balls from the money that the fans sent in, there was still five hundred and forty-one dollars profit!

WE'LL GIVE SAM THE MONEY SHE NEEDS TO PAY US BACK THEN SHE CAN QUIT HER STUPID JOB!

Freddie loved Carly, but he was still taking a while to keep up with the programme.

"Sam's not gonna take any money from us," he argued. "It's a pride thing. That's why she won't quit her job."

"So we find some adult that she doesn't know and we give him five hundred and twenty-six bucks," suggested Carly. "Then he can give Sam the money as a tip in her restaurant!"

Freddie could almost taste the dosh. "That's brilliant! But that leaves an extra fifteen bucks."

"Yeah five for me, five for Sam and five for you," grinned Carly, waving a note in his face.

Go nuts!

"Woo hoo!" screeched Sam, eating chilli straight out of the warming machine. She zig-zagged in and out of the tables, waving the cash like a maniac. She was never doing a day's work in here again!

BABY GOT SOME SUGAR!

Spencer didn't skimp on his celebrations either. He decided to pedal over to see the two sweethearts who'd pinched his spot at the supermarket. "I just wanted you two girls to know that I won the bike," he said soberly. "...and because I'm a grown-up I forgive you for behaving so rudely to me." He pedalled demurely away on Emily's shiny pink BMX. The girls sulked in silence as he disappeared around the corner. They didn't look quite as cool when he cycled back again cheering like a rodeo rider.

"On the other hand," he gabbled. "Check out this cool bike. Yep, I won the fancy new bike and you didn't!"

HOW DO YOU GIRLS LIKE ME NOW?!

Spencer pedalled past the Sunshine Girls' table, tipping it upside down.

"I must be out of control," he smiled. "Oh I'm sorry!"

The girls gasped in surprise, then flushed scarlet. Revenge was indeed a dish best served straight from the fridge!

Sam was in for the greatest shift at Chili My Bowl ever.

Her manager watched as she miserably handed over her hundredth take-out bowl of chilli with extra hot sauce. The customer gave her an envelope, then headed into the night.

Sam stared at the envelope suspiciously – were these nuts sending her hate mail now? She slid the envelope open, then rubbed her eyes.

"Oh, oh look!" she screamed, running her fingers through the packet of twenty dollar bills. "I got money!"

Before the manager knew it his degenerate employee was dancing on the counter.

iOwe YOU

The next day at school Sam couldn't wait to share her news.

"What goes on peoples?" she grinned, dancing in the corridor.

Carly and Freddie acted dumb.

"Hey," smiled Carly. "Where've you been?"

Sam flashed her the biggest grin ever. "I kinda came into a little money. Like five hundred and twenty-six dollars worth!"

Freddie punched the air, the sting had so worked!

"Sooo…" he cooed. "Where is it?"

Sam shrugged with happiness. "I spent it!"

THAT TEARS IT!

Freddie and Carly were floored. This was so not in the grand plan!

"You were supposed to pay us back!" snapped Carly.

Freddie punched his locker. "You're insane."

"I may be insane," conceded Sam. "But I bought something that's gonna be a lotta fun for all three of us."

HOLY CHIZ ON A CHIZEL!

Spencer got the shock of his life when he got home from mouthing off to the Sunshine Girls.

"Hey bro!" shouted Carly. "We're bouncing!"

There, taking up almost the whole apartment, was the biggest trampoline ever. For once Sam had been right, she had bought something that all three of them would enjoy.

Spencer only had one thing to say: "Where's the couch?"

lol

MESSIN' WITH LEWBERT!

You couldn't get a more ridiculous doorman than Lewbert. He has a gigantic wart, a whiny voice and a tendency to kick things if too many people walk into his lobby! Here are some of the gang's favourite Lewbert gags – just make sure you don't repeat any of them if you're in the vicinity of Bushwell Plaza!

Freddie: How many rotten eggs does it take to make a stink bomb to freak out Lewbert?
Sam: A phew!

Mrs. Benson: Why does the Space Needle stand in the centre of Seattle?
Lewbert: Because it can't sit down!

Q: Why did Freddie put the lobby lights on?
A: Because Lewbert was so dim!

Carly: This morning Sam gave Lewbert soap flakes instead of cornflakes for breakfast.
Freddie: I bet he was mad.
Carly: Mad? He was foaming at the mouth!

Lewbert: Doctor, doctor, I think I need glasses.
Doctor: I wondered why you walked through the window.

Q: Why did Lewbert stand on his head?
A: His feet were tired!

Q: What did Freddie say to Lewbert?
A: Wart's new?

Lewbert is so dirty, the only time he washes his ears is when he eats watermelon!

LOCKER LETTERS

Principal Franklin is on the warpath this morning and his target is Sam Puckett! Carly needs to get a message to her friend before diving into Mr. Devlin's History class. There's just time to stick a message in Sam's locker, giving her the heads up!

Carly and Sam have a secret code worked out for just this kind of emergency. Use the key to unscramble the letters and decipher Sam's message. Can you crack it in less than five minutes?

84 36 104 52 64 60 72 52
16 104 52 28 32 28 48
32 88 88 8 48 24 72 52
76 72 32 48 84 84 72 96 88
— 80 88 28 8 48 24 36
88 12 96 24 32 88 32
36 88 104 92 8

:::KEY:::

A = 104	N = 52
B = 100	O = 48
C = 96	P = 44
D = 92	Q = 40
E = 88	R = 36
F = 84	S = 32
G = 80	T = 28
H = 76	U = 24
I = 72	V = 20
J = 68	W = 16
K = 64	X = 12
L = 60	Y = 8
M = 56	Z = 4

Franklin, Wants, To, See, Y__
__/___/_____ ___
_____,_____,____!

WHAT'S YOUR ROLE ON THE SHOW?

HOW WOULD YOU LIKE TO GET INVOLVED IN THE ICARLY WEBSHOW? YOU DON'T HAVE TO BE A STAGE SCHOOL PROTÉGÉ TO MAKE IT AS PART OF THE TEAM, PRESENTING IS JUST ONE ROLE THAT EVERY SUCCESSFUL WEBSHOW NEEDS. CHOOSE ONE OF THE THREE STARTING POINTS THEN TRACE YOUR WAY THROUGH THE CHART, ANSWERING TRUE OR FALSE TO EACH STATEMENT. WHEN YOU GET TO THE END YOU'LL DISCOVER WHAT YOU COULD BRING TO A PRODUCTION OF ICARLY!

START

I like being the centre of attention.

I'll give anything a try once.

I'm happiest keeping a low profile.

I've got a knack for making people laugh.

I'm happy to share the limelight.

My pranks are legendary.

I love being part of a team.

I am a self-confessed show-off.

When I get the giggles I can't stop.

I was born to perform.

I could ad lib all day.

I always turn up for rehearsals.

Singing and dancing makes me cringe.

I'm great at technical stuff.

There is no show without the backroom team.

FALSE · TRUE

60

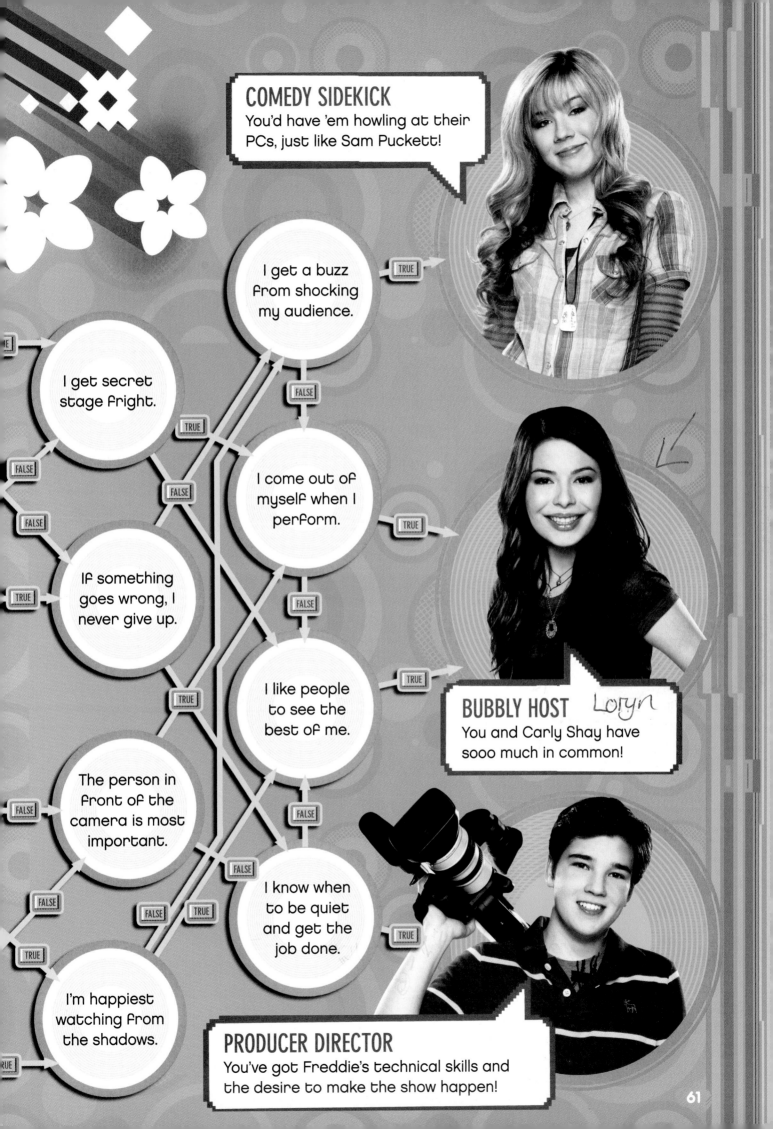

COMEDY SIDEKICK
You'd have 'em howling at their PCs, just like Sam Puckett!

I get a buzz from shocking my audience.

TRUE

I get secret stage fright.

FALSE

TRUE

FALSE

FALSE

TRUE

If something goes wrong, I never give up.

I come out of myself when I perform.

TRUE

FALSE

TRUE

FALSE

I like people to see the best of me.

TRUE

BUBBLY HOST *Loryn*
You and Carly Shay have sooo much in common!

The person in front of the camera is most important.

FALSE

FALSE

FALSE

FALSE

TRUE

FALSE

I know when to be quiet and get the job done.

TRUE

TRUE

I'm happiest watching from the shadows.

RUE

PRODUCER DIRECTOR
You've got Freddie's technical skills and the desire to make the show happen!

SAM'S SPICY BLOG!

'SCUSE ME IF I DRIBBLE WHILE I WRITE THIS, BUT I WANNA TELL YOU ABOUT SOMETHING VERY CLOSE TO MY HEART – COCONUT CREAM PIE.

I was crashing over at Carly's when Spencer decided to take us out to Galini's for breakfast. Galini's is only the greatest pie shop in the northern hemisphere, if not the world! Being a DWEEB, Freddie hadn't heard about the place. It was time for him to get an education!

The pies were awesome as ever, but the waiter Mario told us that the owner, old Mr. Galini, had checked into the hospital. As predicted, Freddie was hooked after the mouthful, just as we got the news that Mr. G had gone up to the big pie shop in the sky. Sure it was sad, but at ninety-seven, the old guy had had a good run. What totally CUT ME UP though, was the news that he'd died without telling ANYONE the recipe for his Coconut Cream masterpiece.

We'd have done anything to get our hands on that recipe. Spencer tried dating Mr. Galini's grim granddaughter Trudy, but even she didn't know the secret! Carly and I launched an appeal on the webshow asking viewers to help us out. I tried sooo many pies that weekend, but didn't get one mouthful of Mr. Galini's magic!

Things got so desperate, we ended up crashing the great man's memorial service. OK, it was a kinda of a SKEEVY thing to do – but we HAD to have that recipe! While Carly and Spencer caused a (very weird) diversion at the wake, Fredward and I crept into the backroom behind the pie shop. We were fighting over Mr. G's PC when his computer sort of got knocked onto the floor! A whole batch of RECIPE CARDS fell out the back of the machine. Trudy and Mario were made up and so were we – the best pie shop in the world was back in business!

Sam x

WHAT, I GOTTA FINISH CHEWING BEFORE I CAN TALK?

Once you've been to Galini's, all you want to talk about is their insanely good food! Here's some examples of how our chat went after our last trip. All you've got to do is insert one three-letter word.

Let's have _ _ _ for breakfast!

It's a _ _ _ shop, not a church. C'mon!

Isn't one _ _ _ as good as any other _ _ _?

Mmmm. Why can't I marry this _ _ _?

Wake me at a quarter to _ _ _.

TOO EASY? SO WHAT! THIS IS MY QUIZ AND I'M GOING TO DO IT HOW I LIKE!

Urgent Smoothie Situation!

It doesn't take Sam long to land herself in trouble at school, but this week she's kicked off even quicker than usual! She slurped a breakfast smoothie on the way in and covered her timetable with froth. Add the right letters to spell out the lessons that she needs to go today. Got to be quick – class starts in five!

Monday

09.00 M A THS

10.00 SPANISH

11.00 ART

12.00 GEOGRAPHY

13.00 LUNCH

14.00 MUSIC

15.00 GYM

16.00 BIOLOGY

Name Game

Have you got a good brain for names? Put your memory to the test with this iCarly crossword. Every answer features someone from the show – can you crack each clue on the grid?

ACROSS

1. Gibby Gibson's flash middle name.

2. Grouchy teacher at Ridgeway who harbours a special dislike for Freddie.

3. Family name of the owner of Sam's favourite pie shop.

4. Carly and Spencer's surname.

5. The surname of Nevel – iCarly's arch-rival.

DOWN

1. Nickname of Spencer's best buddy.

2. Mrs. Benson's elegant first name.

3. How Principal Franklin likes to be known to his friends.

4. Sam's surname.

5. The first name of Carly's dad, Colonel Shay.

65

iKiss

SAM WAS ALWAYS PULLING PRANKS ON FREDDIE. SO WHEN FREDDIE DECIDED TO TURN THE TABLES WHO KNEW WHAT THE CONSEQUENCES WOULD BE?

Carly was clip-surfing on SplashFace when Freddie barged into the apartment. Fear was etched all over his forehead.

"Is Sam here?" he demanded.

When Carly shook her head, he slammed the door and slid the chain across.

Freddie collapsed onto the couch and sank his head into his hands. Carly waited. This had to be bad.

"I pulled a prank on Sam," he whispered.

"Are you tired of living?" yelped Carly. "Why would you mess with Sam?"

Freddie waved a reeking backpack at her.

"Smell this," he insisted. "Sam put a dead fish in my locker."

Carly was grossed out. "So what did you do to Sam?"

Bang! Bang! Bang!

There were no prizes for guessing who was outside. Freddie's face turned whiter than his vest.

CALL THE POLICE!

"Open up!" roared Puckett, hurling herself against Carly's front door. "Leave me alone Sam!" begged Freddie. "We're even now."

There was a terrible howl and then Sam threw herself against the door one more time, ripping the security chain off in her fury. Carly and Freddie gasped as she stormed into the apartment, dragging Gibby behind her.

"You handcuffed Sam to Gibby?" gasped Carly, trying to understand Freddie's death wish.

"She put a dead fish in my locker," said Freddie weakly.

Sam hauled Gibby across the couch, then lunged at Freddie. She hadn't been this mad in days.

"Gibby's way worse than a dead

fish!" she thundered.

Sam dragged Gibby round and round Carly's apartment.

Freddie knew that he looked like a total woose running away from a girl, but he couldn't help it. He'd been belted by Sam before.

"Gimme the key!" she shouted, holding up her handcuffs.

She was hopping with rage now. Poor Gibby just looked terrified.

"Only if you promise to..." started Freddie, trying to bargain with her.

Sam let out a scream and then pounced. In one fell swoop Freddie was spread-eagled across the kitchen island with an arm pushed up behind his back.

Freddie caved at once. "Just let me up and I'll give you the key!"

He reached into his jeans and pulled out the cuff key. As soon as he was released Gibby ran out of the apartment crying.

I'M GONNA GET YOU. MAYBE NOT TODAY, MAYBE NOT TOMORROW. BUT I WILL...

Freddie couldn't think about Gibby right now. He had his own bacon to worry about.

"C'mon," he begged. "You put a dead fish in my locker. I handcuffed you to Gibby. We're even."

Sam walked right into Freddie's personal space. "I don't play to get even," she muttered darkly.

Sam backed slowly out of the apartment, her eyes fixed on the trembling tech-head.

"I'm gonna get you," she promised. "Maybe not today. Maybe not tomorrow. But I **will** get you."

Freddie inched closer to Carly.

"I'm not s-scared," he stuttered.

As soon as the door slammed behind Sam, Freddie reached across the breakfast bar and grabbed a saucepan.

"Are you gonna throw up in that?" checked Carly.

Freddie headed for the bathroom. "Uh-huh."

iKiss

Later that night, Carly and Sam went out to watch a chick flick. Carly hoped a bit of romance might calm her BFF down.

"How was 'The First Kiss?'" asked Spencer when they got in.

Sam rolled her eyes. "Same as every other stupid teen chick movie ever made."

"Yep," grinned Carly. "It made me embarrassed to be a teen chick."

Sam was hanging up her jacket when she noticed that Spencer had an American football tucked under his arm.

"What's up with that thing?" she asked.

Carly shook her head sadly. "He wants to be a professional football player."

"C'mon," shouted Spencer. "It could happen."

SURE, IF ALL THE OTHER PROFESSIONAL FOOTBALL PLAYERS ARE EATEN BY LIONS

"It's his dream that will never be," explained Carly, reaching for a cream soda.

"Uh-wrong," cut in Spencer. "The Seattle Cobras are holding open try-outs for the first time ever, and I'm going for it."

Sam's look was so withering, Spencer felt he had to prove himself. He marched up to the apartment door and flung it open.

"Throw the ball at me as hard as you can Puckett," challenged Spencer. "I'm gonna run all the way back through. Bet you can't stop me."

Carly was just about to point out that a grown man should be able to beat two ninth grade girls when Sam pelted the ball through the door.

There was a thud and a pained oof! Spencer waddled back looking like he'd just got off a horse.

"Next time could you throw the ball a little higher?" he grimaced.

68

While Spencer nursed his home football injury, the girls went upstairs to hang out on the beanbags. Freddie followed them up a few minutes later – armed with a baseball bat.

"What that for?" asked Carly.

"Nothing," frowned Freddie. "As long as Sam keeps her distance."

"Relax," yawned Sam. "I'm too tired to get you back tonight."

Freddie breathed a major sigh of relief and then slumped down on his beanbag. Carly passed round a bowl of popcorn and spilled all the deets about the cheesefest that was 'The First Kiss.'

"I told you guys that movie was gonna be awful," chuckled Freddie.

"So…" asked Sam, suddenly turning to Carly. "Who was your first kiss?"

"He was called Ben Hoobsher," she finally confessed. "I met him one summer vacation when I was staying at my granddad's."

Freddie laughed.

NOBODY'S LAST NAME
IS HOOBSHER!

"Was it good?" asked Sam. Carly blushed. "Just an average little kiss."

"Ni-ice," grinned Sam. "My first kiss was with Buddy Hinten at a Cuddlefish concert."

Freddie started studying the bottom of his trainers. Sam got to her feet and stretched.

"I'm gonna get us some more snacks," she announced. "Back in five."

iKiss @

Freddie had avoided the question, but Carly was sharp. As soon as Sam was out the door, she shuffled forward on her beanbag.

"So…" she whispered. "Who was your first kiss?"

"You don't need to know," replied Freddie.

Carly scoffed. "I absolutely need to know."

Freddie squirmed, but Carly looked him square in the eye. Both of them were concentrating so hard they didn't hear Sam clatter back up the stairs to get some more money.

Freddie finally cracked. He admitted that he hadn't had his first kiss!

Sam froze on the staircase outside the loft – she couldn't believe what she was hearing!

I'VE NEVER KISSED ANYONE

"What about that rotten girl you dated last year?" demanded Carly. "Valerie. You kissed her, right?"

Freddie groaned. "Only for half a second in front of a bunch of guys. Not a real kiss."

This was major news, but Carly was kind enough to play it down.

"I think it's kind of sweet," she decided.

IT'S NOT SWEET, IT'S LAME

"You gotta swear to me that you won't tell anyone," pleaded Freddie. "Especially Sam."

Carly smiled. "I promise."

Out in the hall, Sam was smiling too. She had just struck prank gold.

The next morning, Carly found Spencer on the couch watching the football game.

"Aren't you supposed to be training for your Seattle Cobras try-outs?"

"I am training," Spencer insisted. "I am watching and learning about football."

Carly shook her head. "I knew you weren't gonna take this seriously."

"I just can't get…" Spencer sighed.

"Off your lazy butt?" suggested his little sis.

Spencer nodded sadly then flopped back onto the couch.

"Right!" announced Carly, prodding Spencer in the stomach. "I'm gonna have to motivate you."

STOP SQUISHING IT!

As they didn't have any gym equipment, the Shays got creative. Carly found an old wheelbarrow, jumped in, then got her brother to push her round and round the apartment. It was time for Spencer to build some muscle!

"Is that all you got?" bawled Carly through a loudhailer.

"Man this is too much!" bawled Spencer.

"How long have I been running?"

Carly checked her stopwatch.

"One minute and forty-five seconds," she yelled. "Keep going!"

"But it's just so boring going round in circles," complained Spencer, wringing the sweat off his T-shirt.

Carly gave him the meanest look she could muster.

"You wanna spice things up?" she snarled. "Then drag this thing up the stairs!"

Spencer grabbed the handles and started to pull.

COME ON!

iKiss

LAST WEEK FREDDIE HANDCUFFED ME TO A NERD

'First Kiss' might have been a rotten movie, but it made a great spoof on the iCarly webshow.

Carly and Sam starred in the mock trailer of a new chick flick. Sam played the über-cool, bitchy girl – Carly played the ditzy nice girl who just wants to be popular. Gibby was drafted in to play the love interest.

Freddie rolled the cameras, chuckling at the send-up.

When they'd finished, Sam pressed her sound effects button and Carly announced the end of the show.

"Wait folks!" cried Sam, talking over her. "You know our technical producer Freddie, right?"

Freddie waved hi, unsure what she was up to.

Carly started to look nervous as Sam pulled the camera closer towards her. The show should have closed two minutes' ago and they were still live on air!

"Guess what?" said Sam. "Freddie's never kissed a girl. Neh-ver. Not once. I heard him say so myself and Carly's my witness."

With that bombshell, Sam walked out of the room. A stunned silence hung in the air behind her.

"Don't worry Freddie, it's no big deal," gasped Carly. Freddie dropped his camera and ran after Sam. The next day, Carly had to drag Freddie into school. Literally.

"I don't wanna be here," groaned Fred, pulling down his dark glasses. He'd even tried to disguise himself with a wig and a crazy shirt – anything to avoid the shame.

"You can't ditch school," urged Carly. "You're being way too dramatic about this."

Freddie let himself be pulled over towards the lockers. He was almost ready to take off his insane disguise when a group of tenth grade guys strolled by.

"It's Benson!" leered one. He started doing kissing noises on his hand. Soon everyone in the group was at it too.

Freddie rested his case.

THIS ISN'T A LOOK. IT'S JUST MY FACE

Just then Freddie's history teacher, Mr. Devlin, caught a glimpse of him. Devlin coughed awkwardly, then called Freddie over.

"I don't mean to be rude," he began. "But I hear that you've never kissed a girl."

Freddie turned a whole new shade of red.

"Well thanks for stopping by," said Carly grimly, trying to lead Freddie away.

Mr. Devlin pulled them back, keen to share a few pearls of wisdom.

"You need to face the world with shoulders cocked and say…," the teacher drew breath then blurted out at the top of his voice, "'I'm Freddie Benson, and I have never kissed a girl!'"

The entire hall stopped to cheer and clap. Soon even groups of sixth graders had started pointing and giggling.

"Can I go home now?" begged Freddie.

Carly was defeated. "I would."

iKiss

After school Gibby banged on Carly's front door.

"Hey," said Spencer, opening up. "Carly's not home yet."

"I know," grinned Gibby. "She sent me here." Spencer looked confused.

"I know she was supposed to help you train this afternoon for your football try-outs," said Gibby. "Well she had something to do so she sent me."

Carly's nerdy classmate held up a long list of instructions. His sis had really put some thought into this!

"That's really nice of you, but I decided that I'm gonna bail on the whole Cobras thing," explained Spencer.

YOU RUN ALONG AND DO WHATEVER IT IS THAT GIBBYS DO

Gibby was thrown for a moment. But just as Spencer was gently ushering him back out of the door, he picked up a beaker and chucked it at the athlete's face.

"Carly said in her notes that if you try to be lazy I should throw a cup of water at you," said Gibby, scanning through the list.

"Right!" barked Spencer, wiping his eyes. "Well that was hot coffee."

Gibby scratched his head. "Look I promised Carly that I'd work out with you."

Instead of getting mad, Spencer decided to give Gibby what he wanted. He called the elevator and bundled Gibby inside.

"Let's go for a run in the park across town," smiled Spencer, popping a ten-dollar bill in Gibby's top pocket. "You take a bus and I'll run there. See ya!"

Problem solved.

TRUST ME, THIS IS A GREAT PLAN

A few hours later and Carly was getting ready to go live on air. When they'd originally planned it, this webshow was set to be one of the best. She, Sam and Freddie's friends had been working a new comedy meatball routine, but for the first time ever she wasn't in the mood for goofing around.

"Sorry I'm late!" said Sam, breezing in at the last minute. "Where's Fred-weird?"

Carly didn't look up. "He's not coming."

"What? He stayed home from school all week, he missed two rehearsals and now the show?" Sam raised her eyes. "That's so unprofessional."

Carly couldn't bear it any longer. It was time to tell Sam Puckett a few home truths.

"You really hurt him!" she shouted. "Y'know he won't even talk to his mum? He just sits on the fire escape alone, 'cos he's too embarrassed to see anyone."

YOU RUINED HIS WHOLE LIFE AND YOU DON'T EVEN CARE

"All right," sighed Sam. "I'll go and apologise."

"You went too far this time!" answered Carly. "And you can't fix it. You can't take back what you said."

She checked her Pear Phone. It was time to start the show.

"How can I go live on the Web now that you made me feel all depressed?" demanded Sam.

"I dunno," snapped Carly. "Just get in front of the camera and do it."

iKiss

Carly got behind Freddie's tech station and cued the show in. Despite being bummed, she and Sam tried to pull-off upbeat as best as they could. It just felt so weird not having Freddie dropping in special effects and grinning behind the camera.

"And now for the moment that you've all been waiting for," announced Carly. "Sam and I are about to have our very first..."

"MEATBALL WAR!!" the girls both bellowed as loud as they could.

Sam suddenly flicked off the audio laughter.

"Um... before we start," she said quietly. "I wanna say something."

Carly stood back so her best friend could take centre stage.

"On the last iCarly, I told you guys that Freddie never kissed anyone. And that was really personal, and I shouldn't have said it. And for all you people out there who've been teasing Freddie about it, lay off 'cos I bet a whole lotta you haven't kissed anyone either."

Sam apologised, honestly and from the heart. Her voice tailed off at the end of her speech, when she added quietly, "Including me."

Carly gasped, staggered by the revelation.

"So if you want tease someone about it, tease me," concluded Sam. "Which is a bad idea unless you live near a hospital."

Carly flicked a switch and a crazy photo hit the website.

"Why'd you stop the show?" asked Sam.

"That was amazing," gushed Carly. She was amazed that her friend had claimed she hadn't been kissed so that people would stop teasing Freddie.

"Lying so that people would stop teasing Freddie," said Carly.

Sam looked at the floor. "I didn't lie."

"Seriously?" said Carly, her jaw dropping like a stone.

Sam stuffed a couple of meatballs into her pocket, then headed next door. She needed to talk to Freddie.

76

Sam found Freddie where he'd mostly been for the last week – outside on the fire escape.

"What's up?" asked Sam, taking a bite out of a meatball.

"That was really brave," he said quietly. "What you said."

Sam spotted Freddie's laptop on the floor – she should have known he wouldn't have missed iCarly!

She took a deep breath and apologised again for everything. Not just the kissing thing – all the pranks she'd ever played at his expense. It took some time.

I'M STILL GONNA MESS WITH YOU. I'M JUST GONNA APOLOGISE EVERY FEW YEARS SO I CAN START AGAIN

Freddie smiled and accepted the apology. Heck, it was almost like they were friends!

"People get all freaked out about this kissing thing," groaned Sam. "Sometimes I just wish that I could get it out of the way."

Freddie nodded and chuckled. He prepared for the worst!

"Should we… kiss?" he wondered.

Sam clarified. "You mean, just to get it over with?"

SWEAR THAT WE GO RIGHT BACK TO HATING EACH OTHER AFTER IT'S OVER

Freddie leant in for a kiss – this was too creepy for words! But weirdly, strangely, bizarrely, it actually felt quite nice.

"Good work," mumbled Sam afterwards.

"Thank you," said Freddie, clearing his throat. "You too."

Sam climbed back over the fire escape. She looked back one last time, her face breaking into a broad grin.

Hey," she beamed. "I hate you."

Freddie smiled right back. "I hate you too."

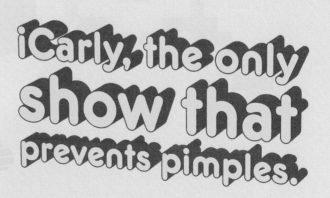

iCarly, the only show that prevents pimples.

Pic-a-Pen
Desk Furniture!

Embrace your inner daffodility with this awesome pencil holder featuring all your best friends! Even Sam is more inclined to do some schoolwork when she has this make-it on her desk. To get started you'll need access to your PC and scanner, plus a stack of your favourite photos.

WHAT YOU NEED: ▁ ☐ ✕

- Blank A4 photo copier paper
- Scissors
- Paper glue
- Empty 400g tin can with a rounded lip
- Brown cardboard
- Ruler
- Glossy photo paper

1. Arrange your favourite pictures in a collage on a landscape sheet of white paper. Trim the photos out, adding extra shots until the paper is completely covered with images.

2. Carefully glue each picture in position then let the collage dry.

3. Ask an adult for permission to scan the collage in so that it becomes one big A4 picture.

4. Take a clean, empty tin can. Wrap the can in a layer of cardboard, using strong paper glue to hold it in place. Trim off any excess card.

5. Use a ruler to measure the height of the can.

6. Hop back on the PC and shrink your photo collage down so that it is 1cm taller than your new pencil pot.

7. Load your computer printer with photo paper and print the reduced collage out. Snip 1cm slots all along the bottom of the collage.

8. Turn the collage over and then cover it with paper glue. Make sure that the cut tabs are also dotted with glue.

9. Wrap the collage around your can, trimming off any excess paper at the end. Gently fold the tabs up underneath the base so that they are stuck in place.

10. Put your designer pot on your desk and then wait for the compliments to roll in!

Design Your Own Poster

Carly needs to get some extra publicity for her webshow, but Spencer's too busy to help out! Can you design an awesome poster that she can stick all over Ridgeway High? Use bright colours to create something so eye-catching that no self-respecting surfer will be able to resist logging on!

You've Got Talent

The iCarly viewers are always astounding Carly and co with their wacky and wonderful clips. A small percentage of them are too out-there for words, but that's the beauty of the show – weird is always welcome! Carly, Sam and Freddie get sent in a ton of stuff every week. To get a place on the show, clips have to get the crew giggling or make their jaws drop to the floor. Can you do something surreal or silly? Use our alphabet ideas guide to help you discover the hidden talent you never knew you had.

Animal-tamer
Train your pet goldfish to swim through hoops or persuade your cat to change channel on the remote control.

Belly dancer
Expose your midriff and show the camera some eye-popping stomach action!

Comedian
Tell your own gags or star in a sketch. Carly and Sam's Cowboy and the Idiot Farm Girl went down a storm!

Drag artist
Swap clothes with your brother or sister. You could even try impersonating your class teacher.

Extreme makeover person
Transform a friend using costumes, props and comedy make-up. Spencer is very proud of his baby makeover.

Fire eater*
Any kind of circus act goes down well on iCarly. If this seems too much of a stretch, give fortune-telling a try.

Game show host
Spoof game shows can be hilarious! Do you remember the iCarly phenomenon 'Guess What I'm Licking?'

Hula-hooper
Grab a ring and get spinning! You'll need to find an unusual location to make your clip stand out from the crowd.

Illusionist
OK, OK, so this is just a flash word for Magician, but the 'M' space was already taken!

Juggler
Forget beanbags or tennis balls, think nappies, crisp packets or bicycle pumps.

Kamikaze go-karter*

Get in your kart and throw a few stunts for the camera!

Mime artist

Act out the Robot, belt out an opera number or score a match-winning goal – all without making a sound.

Outdoor chef

Celebrity chefs are everywhere. Let's see some campsite cooking with an iCarly spin.

Quick drawer

Can you doodle against the clock? Do a comedy caricature good enough to get Spencer begging for art classes!

Silly string entertainer

How can you amuse with a can of silly string? Get out there and find out!

Upside-down eater*

Throw a headstand and then ask a pal to feed you. Try and avoid throwing up on camera.

World-record breaker

Be the best in the world at something new and unique – the dafter the better.

Yo-yo spinner

Practise makes perfect here. Yo-yo until you drop, then synchronise a spinning routine.

Look-a-likie

Are you the spitting image of a famous artist? Whack on a costume and do an impression!

Novelty nail painter

Who knows how far you can push the boundaries with this under-developed art form?

Plate balancer**

Get some sticks twirling, but don't use your mum's best china.

Random dancer

When it comes to this category, the iCarly crew think they have seen it all. Prove them wrong.

Tumbler

Put on a gymnastics display that will get your audience wincing in surprise!

Ventriloquist

Take your annoying little sister's cuddly toy hostage and then give it its own true voice.

Xtreme trampoliner*

Jump around in silly clothes or leap on the grass using an invisible trampoline.

Zzzz... snore musician

Can you make weird and wonderful music through your nose? Perfect the act of snoring to music!

* This stuff could be dangerous! Don't do anything so silly that it could get you hurt or cause any kind of injury. If in doubt, check with someone responsible.

** Almost certain to land you in big trouble. Keep the plates plastic to avoid being grounded forever.

FREDDIE'S awesome BLOG!

Address ▼ → Go

I'M ALWAYS UP FOR A JOKE, but recently we took messin' with LEWBERT up to a whole new level! When a couple of my friends at the AV club worked out how to rig a muffin basket up with a confetti cannon, I was so STOKED that I decided to trial it out on iCarly. Hands up, it wasn't one of my better ideas.

I set up the Lewbertcam in the downstairs lobby, then waited for him to take the bait. The muffin basket worked like a dream in the lab, how was I to know that it was going to explode in the doorman's face? The minute that Lewbert put his hand in the basket, his wart got blown clean of!

I was FREAKED OUT – sure he's the meanest, nastiest doorman in the world, but I didn't plan to put him in hospital because of it!

I breathed a major sigh of relief when we found out that Lewbert was just going to need a week's bed rest to get over the whole thing. While Spencer filled in for him in the lobby, my mum ended up nursing Lewbert back to health. For a time it was the best – Mum was so busy shaving Lewbert's back and scratching his itches with a fork (ulch!) she let me do anything I wanted.

I went WILD! I walked around wearing open-toe shoes, didn't bother putting on my belt and one time I even went to sleep in just my socks!

I was pushing my new freedom to the MAX, when Carly pointed out that Lewbert and my mum loved hanging out together a little too much. The thought of Mum and that nasty man dating totally FREAKED me out! It was time to wake up and smell the boyfriend – this was SERIOUS CHIZZ! Drastic times called for drastic measures.

I faked a tumble down the stairs and got my mum back! Mum was sure I'd only fallen because of my open-toe shoes. When Lewbert didn't show me any sympathy she dropped him like a bad smell. That's a near miss I won't forget in a hurry!

Freddie x

The iCarly crew can't resist a photo booth! We piled into this one the other day at the mall. Sitting that close to Sam was torture, but at least Carly's putting an arm around me (sort of)! One or two of these pictures are an exact match – can you circle them with a pen or pencil?

A

B

C

D

E

F

CLEVER CAPTIONS

CARLY LOVES MAKING SCRAPBOOKS TO SHOW HER DAD WHEN HE COMES HOME ON LEAVE. SHE'S STUCK OF HER RECENT FAVOURITES INTO THIS PAGE, BUT RUN OUT OF TIME TO CAPTION THEM ALL. CAN YOU DO THE JOB FOR HER? FINISH OFF THE PHOTO ALBUM BY WRITING A CAPTION UNDERNEATH EACH SNAP. CARLY'S DONE THE FIRST ONE.

Me with Sam and Freddy just before a night out at our favourite pizza restaurant — check out Sam's grinny smile!

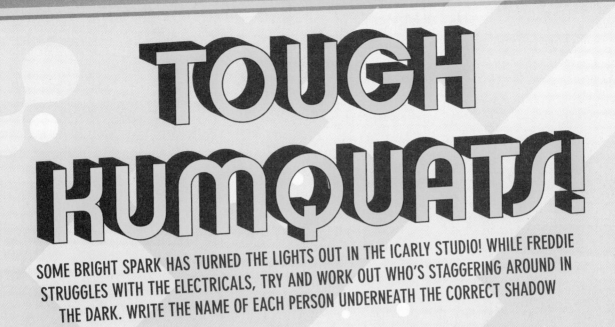

TOUGH KUMQUATS!

SOME BRIGHT SPARK HAS TURNED THE LIGHTS OUT IN THE ICARLY STUDIO! WHILE FREDDIE STRUGGLES WITH THE ELECTRICALS, TRY AND WORK OUT WHO'S STAGGERING AROUND IN THE DARK. WRITE THE NAME OF EACH PERSON UNDERNEATH THE CORRECT SHADOW

A

B

C

It's Art, OK!?!

After quitting law school, Spencer opted for a wackier career. Now he's an avant-garde modern artist with a talent for making sculptures that are full of surprises! He's heavy on talent but light on health and safety — more works that he cares to admit to have exploded or gone up in flames. Here Spencer presents a summary of his finest pieces. Can you match up the art with the right descriptions? Study, savour and enjoy, then draw a line to connect the title with the correct caption.

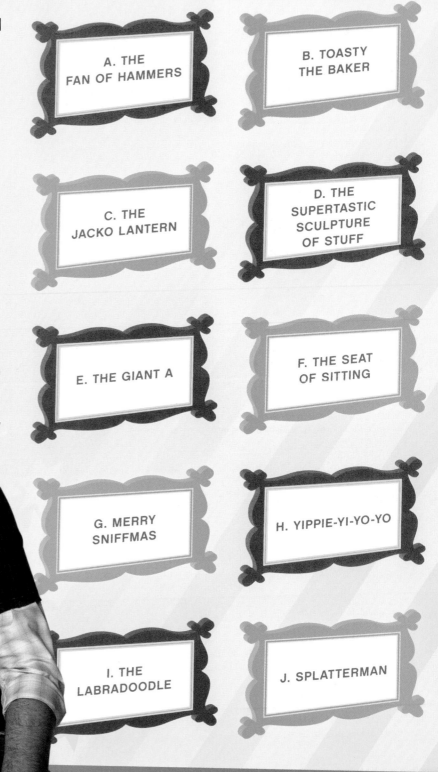

A. THE FAN OF HAMMERS

B. TOASTY THE BAKER

C. THE JACKO LANTERN

D. THE SUPERTASTIC SCULPTURE OF STUFF

E. THE GIANT A

F. THE SEAT OF SITTING

G. MERRY SNIFFMAS

H. YIPPIE-YI-YO-YO

I. THE LABRADOODLE

J. SPLATTERMAN

1. TO CREATE THIS PIECE, CARLY HELPED ME SPRAY MULTI-COLOURED PAINTS OVER A HEADLESS MANNEQUIN. THIS WAS PIECE WAS UNUSUAL IN THAT IT TOOK LONGER TO CLEAN UP AFTER THAN CREATE.

2. WHEN I TRIED TO DO MY OWN TAKE ON THE CLASSIC CHRISTMAS TREE, THE LAST THING THAT CARLY EXPECTED WAS A SPRUCE COVERED IN PLASTIC NOSES!

3. GRANDAD SHAY WAS SPEECHLESS WHEN I FINALLY GOT THIS MOVING SCULPTURE WORKING. UNFORTUNATELY CARLY ALSO NEARLY ENDED UP WITH A TOOL IN HER HEAD.

4. THIS ELECTRIC SCULPTURE WON A WORLD RECORD FOR HAVING THE MOST MOVING PARTS. IT WAS COVERED WITH A MYRIAD OF WIRES AND HOUSEHOLD OBJECTS.

5. I CREATED THIS PIECE IN CELEBRATION OF CARLY'S FULL SET OF TOP MARKS AT SCHOOL. WHAT I DIDN'T REALISE AT THE TIME WAS THAT MY SIS HADN'T QUITE HIT THE GRADE AVERAGE SHE WANTED.

6. I WAS COMMISSIONED BY AN EMINENT SEATTLE RESIDENT TO CREATE THIS SCULPTURE AS A TRIBUTE TO A BELOVED PET.

7. THIS DARING PIECE OF FOOD SCULPTURE ONLY HAD A SHORT LIFE SPAN. NOT ONLY WAS IT HARD TO TRANSPORT, IT WAS ALSO MADE COMPLETELY OUT OF BUTTER.

8. I TURNED A PLAYGROUND CRAZE INTO AN ART FORM WHEN I PUT THIS SCULPTURE TOGETHER. HUNDREDS OF CLASSIC KIDS' TOYS WERE DANGLED FROM A METAL TREE.

9. THIS GIANT CARVING WAS COMPLETED FOR HALLOWE'N. I HAD TO TAKE SHELTER INSIDE IT WHEN A GANG OF JUVENILE TRICK OR TREATERS ATTACKED ME.

10. IT'LL NEVER REPLACE THE SHAY FAMILY COUCH, BUT THIS INSTALLATION WAS ONE OF MY MOST PRACTICAL WORKS OF ART TO DATE.

SUPER FAN QUIZ

PART TWO

QUESTION 11 — □ ✕

Why is Sam's favourite colour brown?

HOLY FLAB!

QUESTION 12 — □ ✕

Who did Carly choose as her date in iSpeed Date?

QUESTION 13 — □ ✕

When Spencer's art idol criticises his sculptures, what job did he do instead?

PANTALONES!

QUESTION 14 — □ ✕

What's the name of Carly, Fred and Sam's bagpipe-playing English teacher?

OK, so you survived Part I, can you get through all of Part II? iCarly aficionados get ready – some of these questions are tougher than a two-dollar steak! Work through the quiz and then add up your scores at the end.

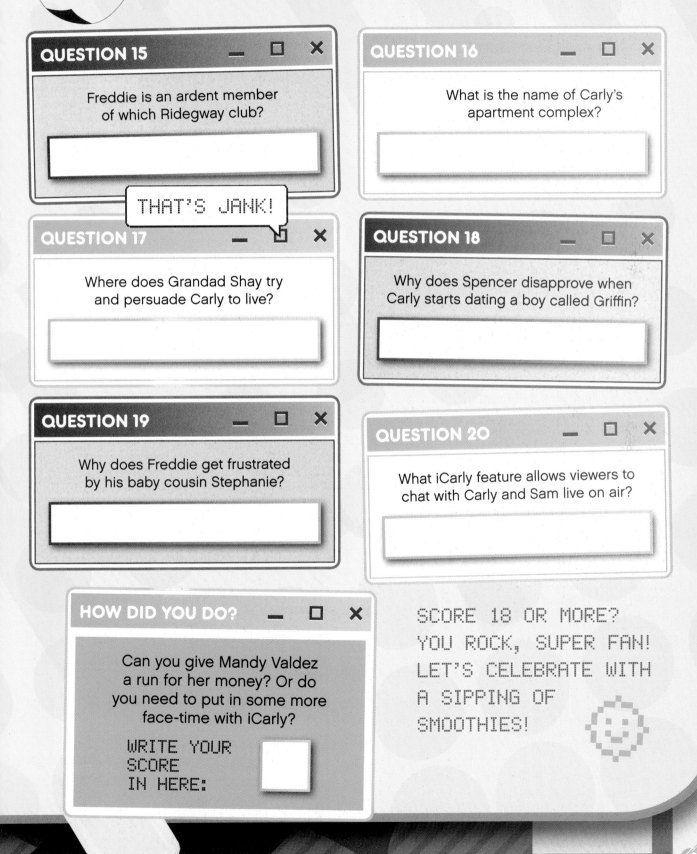

QUESTION 15 — □ ✕

Freddie is an ardent member of which Ridegway club?

QUESTION 16 — □ ✕

What is the name of Carly's apartment complex?

THAT'S JANK!

QUESTION 17 — □ ✕

Where does Grandad Shay try and persuade Carly to live?

QUESTION 18 — □ ✕

Why does Spencer disapprove when Carly starts dating a boy called Griffin?

QUESTION 19 — □ ✕

Why does Freddie get frustrated by his baby cousin Stephanie?

QUESTION 20 — □ ✕

What iCarly feature allows viewers to chat with Carly and Sam live on air?

HOW DID YOU DO? — □ ✕

Can you give Mandy Valdez a run for her money? Or do you need to put in some more face-time with iCarly?

WRITE YOUR
SCORE
IN HERE:

SCORE 18 OR MORE?
YOU ROCK, SUPER FAN!
LET'S CELEBRATE WITH
A SIPPING OF
SMOOTHIES!

iGive AWAY A CAR

Giving away a car on the iCarly show sounded like the coolest thing ever! How could the guys have guessed that it was a disaster waiting to happen?

Freddie and Sam were getting ready to play Cupcake Slam in Carly's kitchen. The rules of the game were simple – grab a cupcake, dip it in icing, then fling it against the door. The cupcake that falls off first loses!

"Ooh, I wanna play!" grinned Carly, picking out a cupcake.

Sam pointed to an old jar that once held gherkins.

"The loser has to drink this pickle juice," she warned.

Freddie took his place in front of the door. At the count of three, the pals hurled their cupcakes.

I FEEL LIKE I'M WATCHING A DVD OF DORKS GONE WILD!

The guys cheered like maniacs until Sam's cupcake fell on the floor with a satisfying *splat!* Freddie and Carly touched knuckles, while Sam poured herself a pickle juice.

Sam downed the drink in one. Freddie was grossed out, but Puckett actually seemed to like it.

Before they could have a re-run, Spencer bounced into the kitchen carrying his Peartop computer.

"Look at this!" he shouted, flipping up the laptop's screen. An auction site revealed a picture of a proton cruiser – a genuine prop from Spencer's favourite movie, *Galaxy Wars*.

Spencer announced that he had just bought it. Freddie did the *Galaxy Wars* handshake with him, totally psyched by the news.

"Wow," said Sam dryly. "I feel like I'm watching a DVD of Dorks Gone Wild."

There was a loud rap on the door. The gang were expecting some interesting company. Carly ran over to open up.

"Hey," said the teenage guy, waiting in the hall. "I'm Jeffrey Flanken."

Carly smiled and showed him inside.

"This is the guy whose father owns Flanken Motors," she explained to Spencer.

"Oh yeah!" remembered Sam. "Doesn't your dad want to set up some kind of contest on iCarly?"

"If you guys are into it," nodded Jeffrey.

Spencer tore his eyes away from his new proton cruiser for a nanosecond to say hi, and then spun the laptop round for Jeffrey to admire his new purchase.

LOOK AT MY SPACESHIP!

Carly rolled her eyes. Jeffrey acted sort of impressed, but she could tell that he thought that Spence was more than a little bit freaky.

"Let's go up to our studio and talk," she hastily suggested.

Freddie, Carly and Jeffrey headed upstairs, but Sam held back for a moment. While they did the introductions, she wanted to have another swig of that pickle juice! Spencer watched aghast as she necked the entire contents of the gherkin jar. Her stomach had to be lined with steel!

REC ●

"My dad wants the contest to be a brainbuster," replied Jeffrey. "Something that you really have to figure out."

"Oh!" cut in Freddie. "You mean like 'how many of Sam's relatives are on parole?'"

Sam kicked him in the shins. "Don't go bagging on my Aunt Maggie, Cousin Garth and Uncle Morris, all right?"

Carly called for order, praying that her friends' squabbles wouldn't make Jeffrey back out of the contest idea. This comp could get the webshow a whole lot of buzz!

"We're in!" she announced. "We'd love to do the give-away-a-car contest."

Sam, Carly and Freddie listened carefully as Jeffrey explained the brainteaser that his dad had set.

"A cowboy rides into town on Friday. He stays in town for three days, and then leaves on Friday. How did he do it?"

Carly shrugged. "I have no idea."

"To keep the contest fair my dad has put the answer in a sealed envelope," said Jeffrey, passing it over.

Carly carefully handed it to Freddie for safe-keeping.

"Why don't you lock this away safely?" she suggested.

Jeffrey's dad had a pretty awesome proposition for the iCarly crew.

"Wait," said Carly, trying to get things straight. "Your dad wants to give away a new car?"

"Yep! He does it once every few years," confirmed Jeffrey. "It's great publicity for his dealership."

"So what kind of competition does he want us to run?" asked Sam.

GUESS THE NUMBER OF
ZITS ON FREDDIE'S BUTT?

MY MUM WANTED A DAUGHTER, OK?

Sam and Carly announced the big car contest on the next episode of the webshow. Now they just had to sit back and wait for the entries to stream in.

Spencer, on the other hand, was more than happy just lovin' his new proton cruiser. He'd had to move the couch and coffee table into storage to fit the craft in, but who cared? Genuine movie artefacts were so much more important than mere furniture.

When no one was looking Spencer couldn't resist flipping the cruiser's communicator and running a few of his favourite quotes.

"This is Commander Spencer," he announced. "A fleet of Red Skynauts has invaded the Alpha Quadrant."

Man he was good at this! Before he knew it, Spencer had hopped into the cockpit to relive a breath-taking battle sequence.

PROTON LASERS SET TO MAXIMOSITY!

Spencer was just about to annihilate the Planet Jooveron when Freddie wandered in.

"I thought you said that this was one of the actual proton cruisers used to film *Galaxy Wars*?" he frowned.

"Uh, it is," replied Spencer.

"Nope," insisted Freddie.

"You're lying," gasped Spencer. "What makes you lie?"

Freddie immediately pointed out at least four things on the cruiser that were never in the movie. The sticker that said 'not an actual prop' was also a bit of a clue. Spencer was devastated.

He'd paid for a real proton cruiser from *Galaxy Wars*, but he'd been fobbed off with a replica!

93

iGive AWAY A CAR

A couple of weeks later there was a real buzz of excitement in the iCarly studio – it was time to announce the winner of the car competition!

"If you have a hat…" began Carly.

Sam grinned. "…you'd better hang on to it…"

"…'cos we're about to give away a brand new car, courtesy of Flanken Motors!"

Freddie cued up a drum roll as Carly carefully opened the envelope with the answer to brainbuster inside.

"I get it!" she cried. "The cowboy can arrive in town on Friday, stay for three days and leave on a Friday because his horse's name is Friday!"

Sam pressed a button on her remote – it was time for a serious dose of random dancing!

WHAT A SHOCK!

Sam checked the monitor to find out which contestant had sent their answer in first. The lucky winner's screen name was Trickster206.

"And now Freddie will connect us to the winner via video chat," revealed Carly.

Sam turned to the flat screen behind them.

"Hey Trickster206," she teased. "Guess what you have won?"

"Would that be a new car?" said a horribly familiar voice.

The friends' mouths hung open – Nevel Papperman's snidey face suddenly appeared on the screen.

"You?" blurted Carly.

"That's right Carly Shay, I won the car," gloated Nevel. "Isn't this delicious?"

I CAN'T BELIEVE THAT NUB WON

The trip to Flanken Motors was set to be such a letdown – where was the fun in helping a winner collect an amazing prize when the winner was your arch-enemy?

"I can't believe that nub won our contest," groaned Sam, walking past the gleaming bonnets in the car showroom.

Sam and Freddie eventually tracked down Jeffrey's dad, Don Flanken. He launched into a slick sales pitch, stopping abruptly when Sam explained that they weren't here as paying customers.

"Your son set up the contest?" she reminded him. "One of our viewers has won a car.

Don looked perplexed.

"I don't have a son," he replied. "I've got two daughters. My oldest Jessica is a bit mannish but…"

Carly interrupted him, shuffling over with an intensely smug Nevel in tow.

THIS NUT-LOAF SAYS HE DOESN'T KNOW ANYTHING ABOUT OUR CONTEST

"I don't have time for this," said Don. "I gotta take my daughter to a doctor."

"Wait!" pleaded Carly, trailing after him. It looked like the car prize was off…

"I entered an online contest and won a car," declared Nevel. "If you don't give me one I'm going to report you to the LCC for fraud."

"Oooo," cooed Carly, putting her 'big deal' face on.

Nevel sneered. "And I'll have iCarly shut down."

"Ooooh!" groaned Carly. It really was a big deal.

iGIVE AWAY A CAR

Back home, Spencer was showing a pair of removal guys where to put the couch. After discovering that his proton cruiser was a fake, he'd decided to put the craft into storage.

"Thanks guys," he said, handing them some cash. It was good to have the sofa back where it belonged.

"You're light," said one of them. "You owe us three hundred bucks."

Spencer semi-choked. They'd said they'd move the spaceship to storage for one hundred dollars!

The removal guy winked at his mate. "The spaceship was a hundred. It's two hundred to bring the couch back."

When Spencer tried to argue, the men picked up the couch and headed back out the door. He didn't have two hundred more, but did they really need to take the chair away again?

THAT'S MY COUCH!

A little later, Carly, Freddie and Sam walked into the hallway. Nevel had been driving them nuts all the way back from the car showroom. If he didn't stop needling at them soon, Sam was gonna snap.

"Where is my car? I don't see a car," whined Papperman. "All I hear is a lot of prattle and..."

Sam snapped. She jumped

on top of the little squirt and wrestled him to the floor. Although it would have been so good to see Sam beat up Nevel, Freddie pulled her off.

"We're not saying that you didn't win the car," argued Freddie.

Carly agreed. "Don't you understand that there's been some kind of mix-up?"

Nevel brushed himself down, then waved a piece of paper in Carly's face.

"According to section nine of the Internet legislation, any website that engages in fraud will be subject to immediate termination," he spat. "You have forty-eight hours iCarly!"

"Wait a minute," said Freddie. "Why did you have that sheet printed out?"

Nevel waved his hand nervously.

Smoke started to come out of Sam's ears. "You set this whole thing up! You sent that 'Jeffrey' guy to us, didn't you?"

"The clock is ticking," replied Nevel, with a self-satisfied look in his eye.

Carly bundled her friends into the apartment before they were driven to do something else illegal.

IT WAS ALL A SET-UP!

Inside the place looked, well, bare. Spencer was perched on an itty bitty stool in the middle of the room.

"Where'd your proton cruiser go?" asked Freddie.

Spencer sighed. "I paid some mean removal guys to take it into storage."

"OK," said Carly. "So where's our couch?"

Spencer was still feeling touchy. "You know there's more to life than couches OK?!"

iGive AWAY A CAR

REC ●

Carly, Sam and Freddie decided to make some snacks. They were in deep trouble. Maybe pretzels could make them happy again.

"How did Nevel like his car?" asked Spencer.

"There is no car," grouched Sam. "Nevel set us up."

"And if we don't get him one, he's going to go to the LCC, claim fraud and get iCarly shut down," added Carly.

SO GET THE LITTLE TUG-MUNCH A CAR

Freddie necked a soda.

"We can't afford to get the creep a car," he explained, stating the oh-so-obvious.

"Maybe ya can," argued Spencer. "My buddy Socko's got an uncle who sells used ones. I bet he could find you a car, super cheap."

Carly pulled out her phone and got ready to dial.

I DIDN'T COME HERE TO BE INSULTED. I CAME HERE TO GET A CAR

The next day, Nevel rocked up at Bushwell Plaza to claim his winnings.

""Are ya ready?" asked Carly, whisking a sheet off a car-shaped object parked in front of the lobby.

Underneath, was the biggest hunk of rust Nevel had ever seen in his life. The cheapest car that Socko's pal had available.

"What is that poop?" he spluttered. "I figured that you iCarlys would try to pull a fast one."

Carly and her friends were enjoying a rare

moment of triumph when a man with an LCC clipboard suddenly appeared.

Nevel ran straight over and grabbed his arm.

"Look at the automotive abomination these people are trying to foist upon me!" he screeched. "Well I won't have it, I simply won't!"

The man examined the junked-out car. "I reviewed your website and you promised the winner a new car," said the man. "And this is… poo."

Nevel clapped his hands, squealing, "Read them the rules!"

"A new car is defined as quote…" the man cleared his throat. "'A unique vehicle that's never been State registered, and can travel under its own power at a speed of at least twenty-five miles per hour.'"

"C'mon! Can't you give us a break?" begged Freddie.

The man agreed to another twenty-four hours. If Nevel didn't get new wheels by then, iCarly was finished.

"Nevel!" cried Carly. "Why is it your life-long dream to get rid of iCarly?"

Nevel pouted. "It's not."

MY LIFE-LONG DREAM IS TO OPEN MY OWN HABERDASHERY

Freddie was stumped by Nevel's answer. Nevel wanted to open a haberdashery shop. "It's a shop that sells accessories such as buttons, ribbons, zips, sewing needles and cotton!" he rattled.

He could never understand why no one knew that!

Papperman stomped down the road, leaving the reject car rusting in its parking spot.

WINNER SAYS HA. HA!

99

 iGive AWAY A CAR

Sam turned up at Carly's place that evening, hoping her friend would have come up with a brainwave to get them out of this mess.

Spencer answered. Carly was in the shower.

"She's been in there most of the day," he explained. "She takes really long showers when she's depressed.

"Carly!" shouted Sam. "Get out of the shower!"

When there was no answer, she decided to sit it out in front of the TV.

"Hey," she noticed. "You got your couch back."

"The removal guys wanted two hundred bucks," nodded Spencer. "But Socko's cousin only charged me fifty bucks to steal it back!"

At least someone had some good news today.

DO YOU REALLY THINK NEVEL'S GONNA HAVE THE LCC SHUT DOWN ICARLY?

Sam threw herself on the couch in a fit of despair.

"Yep," she grunted. "Unless we can come up with a unique vehicle that's never been State registered and can travel under its own power at a speed of at least twenty-five miles per hour."

"By when?"

Sam sighed. "Tomorrow."

There was a long silence. Spencer stared into the distance, his quirky brain slowly turning.

"I know that look," said Sam. "Are you thinking what I'm thinking?"

Spencer's eyes flashed – he was thinking all right!

"I'm thinking of a way to give Nevel that vehicle," he announced. "Weren't you?"

"Oh, no," answered Sam.

I WAS THINKIN' ABOUT FRIED CHICKEN

Nevel made sure he got to Carly's place extra-early the next morning – he was this close to getting her webshow closed down. The creep wanted to savour every malicious minute.

Spencer and the LCC man waited outside Bushwell Plaza. Carly's big brother had taken the liberty of buying them both ice lollies.

"Mmm…" enthused Spencer. "What is this, pineapple?"

The inspector had another lick. "Maybe mango?"

lol

REC ●

"Will you two shut up?" snapped Nevel.

I'M ABOUT TO RID THE INTERNET OF ICARLY FOREVER AND YOU'RE SPOILING MY MOMENT!

"Hey Nevel," grinned Spencer. "Lookie, lookie."
Nevel clasped his chest in horror as Carly, Sam and Freddie drove into the car park. They were behind the wheel of a fully functioning, brand new car. The model? Proton cruiser.
"Congratulations!" beamed Carly. "Here you go."
"Do you really think that rolling space turd will get you off the hook!" hissed Nevel.
The LCC man ticked a few boxes on his clipboard. This car was new and had clearly never been State registered.

"If it can travel at a speed of at least twenty-five miles per hour, it technically qualifies as a new car," he said.
Before you could say 'haberdashery' Nevel had snatched the keys and climbed into his prize.
"Let's just see if this thing can do twenty-five," he muttered. A few seconds later the gang heard a massive crash! It appeared that the car could.
"Ya think it definitely qualifies?" giggled Carly.
The LCC inspector put away his clipboard.

YOU CAN'T DO THAT KIND OF DAMAGE TO A FLOWER SHOP UNLESS YOU'RE DOING AT LEAST TWENTY-FIVE

"Alright then," replied Sam, basking in the moment. "Let's go get some more of those ice lollies."

SWEET STUDENT SUDOKU

Carly Shay always gets top marks in her maths class, even when she sits next to Sam! Now she's got to put her money where her mouth is – she's challenged Nevel Papperman to a sudoku race. The puzzle is fiendishly difficult. Can you help her crack it?

FILL THE GRID WITH NUMBERS. EACH NUMERAL FROM 1 TO 6 ONLY APPEARS ONCE IN EACH ROW, COLUMN AND RECTANGLE.

				4	3
1			6		
6					4
3			2	5	
	5	6			2
2				5	4

A SNEAK

Low-life doorman Lewbert has been peeping through the keyhole of Carly's front door! Can you work out who he's spotted hanging out inside? Study each of the keyhole sightings, the write the correct name underneath.

1

2

3

4

AMS	DREFIED	LACYR	NERPCES
Sam	Freddie	Carly	Spencer

stumped?

Use the anagram clues to help you unscrabble the answers!

SPENCER'S WEIRD BLOG!

HEY THERE JIGLITS, good to see you've flipped to my blog! You're lucky that there's anything to read on this page, 'cos I have been super busy recently. As well as working on a brand new commission for a Labradoodle sculpture, I've been spending some major face-time with my biggest junkyard haul EVER!

I couldn't believe my luck when I found an old eighties Pak-Rat arcade game in amongst all the RUBBISH at the city dump! I'd played versions of it online before, but this was the real deal! I checked out all the wiring and circuit boards, then cranked up the game. Pak-Rat was one of the most popular video games ever and I wanted to have a piece!

The game totally took over my life. I thought it was a good takeover, but Carly didn't seem to agree. I was doing so well on Pak-Rat, I didn't have time for a bunch of other stuff such as eating, brushing my teeth or answering the door. Pak-Rat was just too much fun to leave! Besides, I had to make the little fella on the screen EAT THE CHEESE!!!

My top score was 867,000, but I wanted more! That's when Carly got in touch with Sacha Striker, the world's number one Pak-Rat player. She figured that if I could beat the champ, I might let the whole Pak-Rat thing go and concentrate on my mixed-breed dog sculpture.

Sacha and I played for six hours straight. The world's geekiest gamers all turned up to watch. This was serious stuff and I was on a ROLL! Carly, Sam and Freddie all went nuts when I beat Sacha's record of 1,320,000 points.

I was so excited I could belly rub! As soon as we finished, the guys herded the gamers out of the front door quicker than you could say 'MAGIC MEATBALL'.

Now it was time to retire from Pak-Rat and get back to that Labradoodle sculpture...

Spencer x

When it comes to gaming, I guess I've got an addictive personality! Carly's so sick of my hobby, she's hidden my brand new game console. Only one of these trails leads to the little beauty, can you help me find it?

A B C

Web Winners

Carly and co think that the Internet is the best thing since fried chicken! When they're not filming their own webshow, they're blogging or looking up cool stuff on SplashFace.

1. www. iCarly.com

2. www. _____

3. www. _____

4. www. _____

5. www. _____

6. www. _____

7. www. _____

8. www. _____

9. www. _____

10. www. _____

Use this page to store your all-time top ten favourite weblinks – we've filled in the first one for you!

Episode Tick Page

THOSE GREAT ICARLY EPISODES KEEP ON COMING!
USE THIS PAGE TO KEEP A RECORD OF ALL THE
SHOWS YOU'VE SEEN IN SEASONS ONE AND TWO.

Season One

1. iPilot ☐
2. iWant More Viewers ☐
3. iDream Of Dance ☐
4. iLike Jake ☐
5. iWanna Stay With Spencer ☐
6. iNevel ☐
7. iScream On Halloween ☐
8. iSpy a Mean Teacher ☐
9. iWill Date Freddie ☐
10. iWant a World Record ☐
11. iRue the Day ☐
12. iPromise Not To Tell ☐
13. iAm Your Biggest Fan ☐
14. iHeart Art ☐
15. iHate Sam's Boyfriend ☐
16. iHatch Chicks ☐
17. iDon't Want To Fight ☐
18. iPromote Tech-Foots ☐
19. iGot Detention ☐
20. iStakeout ☐
21. iMight Switch Schools ☐
22. iFence ☐
23. iCarly Saves TV ☐
24. iWin A Date ☐
25. iHave A Love Sick Teacher ☐

Season Two

26. iSaw Him First ☐
27. iStage An Intervention ☐
28. iOwe You ☐
29. iHurt Lewbert ☐
iGo To Japan TV movie ☐
30. iPie ☐
31. iChristmas ☐
32. iKiss ☐
33. iGive Away A Car ☐
34. iRocked The Vote ☐
35. iMeet Fred ☐
36. iLook Alike ☐
37. iWant My Website Back ☐
38. iMake Sam Girlier ☐
39. iGo Nuclear ☐
40. iDate A Bad Boy (2 parts) ☐
41. iReunite With Missy ☐
42. iTake On Dingo ☐
43. iMust Have Locker 239 ☐
44. iTwins ☐
45. iFight Shelby Marx ☐

ANSWERS!

NEVER IN MY ENTIRE LIFE HAVE I EATEN ONE PAIR OF PANTS.

PAGE 18: PEAR PHONE PUZZLE

1. FREDDIE / 2. SPENCER
3. NEVEL / 4. GIBBY / 5. SAM

PAGE 19: ...IT'S CREDDIE!

PAGES 20-21: CARLY'S HOT BLOG!

1. C / 2. D / 3. B / 4. A

PAGE 36: CHEESE TEASE

GIBBY gets sprayed by Sam.

PAGE 37: CARLY'S WORLD WORDSEARCH

E	I	H	T	O	O	M	S
J	X	N	E	V	E	L	P
A	A	L	L	Q	X	W	E
K	V	D	T	K	B	V	N
E	Y	U	T	C	I	J	C
T	V	S	A	M	S	U	E
Y	A	W	E	G	D	I	R
O	N	G	S	R	H	S	T

1. Carly's big brother is called SPENCER.

2. Carly goes to school at RIDGEWAY High.

3. Carly's dad serves in the US NAVY.

4. Carly and her friends live in SEATTLE.

5. Carly used to have a crush on a hot guy called JAKE.

6. Carly's arch web-rival is NEVEL.

7. Carly's fave drink is a SMOOTHIE.

8. Carly's BFF is called SAM.

PAGES 38-39: SUPER FAN QUIZ PART 1

1. Grubbles / 2. Zaplook
3. Skunk-bag! / 4. Law School
5. Sam Puckett / 6. Galaxy Wars
7. Principal Franklin
8. The Fan of Hammers
9. Melanie / 10. The Blab Cam

PAGE 59:
LOCKER LETTERS

FRANKLIN WANTS TO SEE
YOU IN HIS OFFICE – GET
YOUR EXCUSES READY!

PAGES 62-63:
SAM'S SPICY BLOG!

Add the word PIE
(what else?!) every time.

PAGE 64:
URGENT SMOOTHIE
SITUATION!

09.00	MATHS
10.00	SPANISH
11.00	ART
12.00	GEOGRAPHY
13.00	LUNCH
14.00	MUSIC
15.00	GYM
16.00	BIOLOGY

PAGE 65: NAME GAME

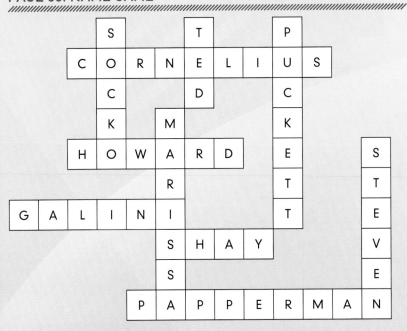

PAGES 82-83:
FREDDIE'S AWESOME BLOG!

PAGE 85:
TOUGH KUMQUATS!

1. Spencer / 2. Carly / 3. Sam

PAGES 86-87:
IT'S ART, OK!?!

A. 3 / B. 7 / C. 9 / D. 4 / E. 5
F. 10 / G. 2 / H. 8 / I. 6 / J. 1

PAGES 88-89:
SUPER FAN QUIZ PART II

11. It's the colour of gravy
12. Austin / 13. A dental assistant
14. Miss Briggs / 15. The AV club
16. Bushwell Plaza / 17. With him
in Yakima / 18. Because he
stole the motorbike that Carly
got him for Christmas
19. Nevelocity.com / 20. He
can't make her laugh or smile

PAGE 102:
SWEET STUDENT SUDOKU

5	6	2	4	3	1
1	4	3	6	2	5
6	2	5	1	4	3
3	1	4	2	5	6
4	5	6	3	1	2
2	3	1	5	6	4

PAGE 103:
ISPY A SNEAK!

1. SAM / 2. FREDDIE /
3. CARLY / 4. SPENCER

PAGES 104-105:
SPENCER'S WEIRD BLOG!

C